A SHAVE AND A KISS

The water was cold, and the soap was a dried-up little cake, so it did not lather quite as well as it should, but soon May was approaching Etienne's lathered chin with the razor, which he had shown her how to strop to sharpness. Her hand was shaking as much as his would be, surely, she thought, but he could not do it for himself without a mirror, and she had neglected to bring that necessary item.

And so she brought up the razor and scraped at his cheek. He stayed steady, his face turned trustingly for her. It took a few minutes but soon she found the rhythm, and exactly how hard to pull to remove whiskers and not skin. Her hands settled as she focused on the task at hand, and finally she was wiping the last flecks of soap from his face.

"I did it," she breathed, rinsing and discarding the razor and gazing at his clean face. The handsome, clean-shaven Etienne she knew had emerged.

He turned toward her, and her heart leapt at the genuine smile of deep appreciation on his face. "Thank you, little . . . Lady May."

Before she recognized his intentions, he had encircled her in his arms and pulled her to him for a kiss. . . .

Books by Donna Simpson

LORD ST. CLAIRE'S ANGEL

LADY DELAFONT'S DILEMMA

LADY MAY'S FOLLY

Published by Zebra Books

Lady May's Folly

Donna Simpson

ZEBRA BOOKS
Kensington Publishing Corp.
http://www.zebrabooks.com

ZEBRA BOOKS are published by

Kensington Publishing Corp.
850 Third Avenue
New York, NY 10022

All Kensington titles, imprints and distributed lines are available at special quantity discounts for bulk purchases for sales promotions, premiums, fund raising, educational, or institutional use.

Special book excerpts or customized printings can also be created to fit specific needs. For details, write or phone the office of the Kensington Special Sales Manager: Kensington Publishing Corp., 850 Third Avenue, New York, NY, 10022, Attn. Special Sales Department. Phone: 1-800-221-2647.

Zebra and the Z logo Reg. U.S. Pat. & TM Off.

First Printing: February, 2001
10 9 8 7 6 5 4 3 2 1

Printed in the United States of America

Prologue

In the quiet darkness of a warm, early autumn night near the Kent coast, the sound of scraping echoed, followed by a muffled groan. Again scraping—the sound of a wounded man inching across a stone floor in a folly set deep in a wooded glade. A young man left a trail of blood as he pulled himself inch by torturous inch over the stone floor and deep into the sanctuary, where he collapsed, wracked by pain. The floor was cool and he laid his fevered cheek against it and wondered if this was where death would finally find him.

He had been many places in the last months; he had been running for his life, but never had he outdistanced those who were after him. He knew that now. He had felt safe in the Widow Jones's arms and bed and within her luscious body, but it had been a fool's comfort, merely an illusion. And for that idiocy he had been stabbed while sleeping in bed, an ignominious fate for a Frenchman. And yet, if one must die . . .

But he was not dead. Not yet. Barely had he gotten away; by inches had he evaded capture, and only because of his stallion, his magnificent friend, Théron.

Surely Delisle would not find him here! Surely the

Lord would protect him, though he was the least worthy of His creations and had many reparations to make in his lifetime before his debt was wiped clean. *Dieu,* but the wound hurt! The pain was a throbbing that shot through his hip. Perhaps he would die now. Brown eyes wide open, glazed by pain and loss of blood, he propped himself up against the wall and probed the wound with his good hand.

Diable! It was like being stabbed all over again was his brief thought, then his eyes closed and he slid down, unconscious, his head hitting the stone floor.

One

Lady May van Hoffen galloped over the dry ground, tall grass whipping around the legs of her mount, Cassiopeia. The dun mare was responsive to her every move, and May, in men's breeches and riding astride as she did in her childhood, felt the elation of sweet freedom throb through her veins. All summer she had indulged her every whim, now that she was free of her mother's machinations and stultifying presence, and slowly she had shed the fears and haunting reminders of a spring spent in the dirty hole that was London. Now, this morning, she felt a new hum of excitement through her veins, a new feeling of liberty and independence.

She could not remember a time when she had felt so at home at Lark House, the residence her father had left her, a rosy-colored brick manse in the countryside near the Kent coast. And yet always, since she had first learned that the house would one day be hers absolutely, she had felt that she *could* be happy there, that it was her home. But not with her mother there. Her father had died when she was just two years old, and in the more than twenty years since then her mother, Maisie van Hoffen—"Lady" van Hoffen, though in her case "Lady" was only a title and not a description—had become notorious among the *ton* for her licentious behavior. Man after man had become her lover. From lords of the realm down to her own footmen, Maisie, a onetime actress plucked from the stage and married by an aging European nobleman in need of an heir, was not particular, as long as they wore breeches.

And May, her only child—not the male heir Lord Gerhard van Hoffen had hoped for—had suffered in every way imaginable. Lark House had been the scene of many of her mother's famous debauched house parties, and from a young age May had known to keep her bedroom door locked and to ignore the sounds coming from the rest of the house. Going off to school had been a sweet relief, but inevitably she had had to come back and take her place in society.

It had been five long, horrible years, living with her mother again after leaving school, but now it was over. Her mother had finally stepped over the line last spring when she tried to sell her daughter in marriage to an elderly roué who needed to breed an heir. The *ton* would have looked the other way, for what young girl did not have to marry sooner or later, someone socially acceptable, meaning of the right lineage? But Maisie's lover, a horrible, smelly, disreputable man who called himself Captain Dempster, had become involved. Old Lord Saunders did not feel himself up to "breaking in," as he had put it, a squeamish virgin. Dempster had volunteered to do the deed.

And so May had suffered through the most frightening night of her life. Kidnapped away from a masquerade ball, where her friend, Lady Emily Delafont, Marchioness of Sedgely, was attempting to speak to May's mother about the impending marriage, she was taken to a remote cottage, where Dempster intended to take her virginity by force. But he had not! No, she had summoned all of her courage and defeated him, and then rode away on a majestic black stallion, sitting in front of the most handsome man she had ever seen in her life, the only man . . .

She turned her thoughts away from a subject that could only bring her pain, and pulled Cassie to a halt. She was at the top of a long rise, still on her own land but a mile or more from the house, which she could barely see in the distance, on another rise. The hillside sloped down to a sweeping panorama of green meadows, lush with late summer wildflowers, and groves of beech and alder, oak and chestnut, trees that had seen centuries come and go. The early morning sunlight slanted across the landscape, sparkling off dew and rising a mist from the grass. Never had she seen anything so beautiful.

She was followed by no groom, and she gloried in the feel of men's breeches clinging to her legs and her horse between her knees, the way God surely meant women to ride. What idiot thought that sidesaddle was in any way comfortable? It was another of those conventions intended to keep women bound and gagged by society, without one iota of the freedom men enjoyed every day of their lives. They misused that freedom to wield power over their wives and daughters, forcing women into stays and sidesaddles and restricting marriages.

But not her. She had finally come to appreciate her freedom after a summer spent searching her soul for answers to what she wanted from life. It was just this; it was merely to ride her land and live free.

This was the farthest she had been alone since com-

ing to Lark House in the spring, a wounded, fright
ened mouse that trembled at the shadow of a hawk.
But she was healing. She was stronger. Now she rode
alone again. Now she felt the throbbing pulse of free
dom in her heart.

She dug in her heels and Cassie bolted. They rode
like the wind down the long sloping sweep of her
land, her home, pins tumbling from her restrained
hair and her auburn-tinted tresses flowing down her
cambric-clad back, tangled curls fluttering in the
breeze. She laughed out loud, thinking what people
would say if they saw her.

She would be taken away to Bedlam! Everyone
thought her so prim and proper, but it was a sham, a
ruse, a cloak she pulled around herself to conceal her
true nature, her wholly inappropriate wildness, from
the *ton*. But here at Lark House, the *ton* did not exist.
Even her friends—Lady Emily, who had been so good
to her, and Lady Dianne Delafont, Dodo as she was
affectionately called, Emily's aunt, who even now
stayed with her as she recovered her equanimity—
even they did not know this side of her.

And never would. No one must ever know the true
self she hid beneath gray gowns and gray shawls, her
hair constricted and tortured into a tight bun, all
spark and spirit in her eyes hidden by the down-sweep
of thick fringed eyelashes. They would turn from her
in disgust and revulsion if they knew that Maisie's
wildness had its form of outlet in May. She might not
be sexually promiscuous, but she hated the strictures
placed on her by society. She was fit only for the coun
try, she thought, pulling her heaving mount to a halt
near a copse of trees deep in the valley, to catch her
breath. She was fit only for the country and her own

company, and she would live out her days at Lark House, trying to help the people of her village in whatever way she could.

She envied women like Emily Delafont, her niece Celestine, and Emily's aunt Dodo Delafont. Those women were all effortlessly ladylike, cultured, womanly. They fit into society like a delicate hand in a lovely kid glove, smoothly and without a wrinkle, and yet were still themselves. They deserved all of the adulation the men around them offered them.

No man would want a woman like her, May thought, stroking Cassie's neck and murmuring to the mare. What man wanted a wild woman, a girl who wore breeches and curried her own horse, who would spend hours—days if she could—in the forest with nature as her only companion? But it was all right. She never wanted to marry. She could not imagine, despite what Emily had told her, letting a man touch her in the intimate ways a man must, to beget a child when he married a woman. Emily had said that it was a beautiful thing, the intimacy between man and woman, but that was ridiculous! It was an animalistic rutting ritual, disguised by society's veneer of chivalrous conduct toward women, a veneer that was stripped away as soon as a man became aroused. No one could tell her differently. No man could ever make *her* want to touch him or . . .

Although . . .

She let Cassie walk and crop the tender shoots of grass near the edge of the wooded copse as she let her mind drift back to Etienne. Etienne Roulant Delafont. If he had not come to rescue her, she might have been taken forcefully by Captain Dempster. She had escaped the captain's grasp by kneeing him, as a

groom of hers once called it, "where it counts." But
Dempster had a gun, and if Etienne—handsome, gallant Frenchman that he was—had not been there with
his magnificent stallion, Théron, she might be lying
under the ground six feet now, instead of riding on
this glorious autumn morning across the grasslands
of her home.

And she never had been able to thank him properly. He was dead. His splendid young life was cut
short in his escape to the Continent—some said he
was responsible for a series of attacks on the Marquess
of Sedgely, her friend Emily's taciturn husband, and
that he was escaping "justice"—when his boat went
down in the channel, near Dover off the Kent coast.
Not far from Lark House, in fact.

She had suffered a piercing pain on hearing about
his death, and it still brought her such great sadness.
She could have loved him like a brother—yes, like a
brother! She told her mind that firmly, though her
brain insisted that the hot feelings that coursed
through her that morning as she rode in front of him
all the way to London were definitely not sisterly. But
she must not dwell on it! She must not linger on the
sweetness of his lilting French voice, his handsome
face, his perfect form. He was the most gorgeous
young man she had ever in her life seen, and now he
was entombed in the frigid depths of the channel. It
was too painful to think about!

A sob caught in her throat. *Etienne,* she thought,
how could your young life be cut so cruelly short? It was not
fair, nor right, nor . . .

Enough! She slid from Cassie's back and wiped the
moisture from her eyes. She led her mare by the bri-
dle, comforted by the soft snuffling of Cassie in her

ear as they entered the cooling shade of the copse. There was a path here somewhere, she thought. . . . Ah, *there* it was. This was the back way into the copse. As a child, mounted on one of Cassie's predecessors, a small shaggy pony she named Jack, she would come this way after escaping from the groom who was supposed to be riding with her. She and Jack would wander through the woods—a forest that seemed deep and dark then, but was really a light-filled, planned glade—and she would come to the . . . oh, yes! There it was, just ahead!

She stopped and swept her tumbled mane of curls back. The folly! She had almost forgotten its existence, but there it was, her fairy castle in her youth, her perfect hideaway. She would ride Jack into the woods, carrying pilfered fruit and meat pies wrapped in paper, and she would spend the day in the folly. Mother would be busy with her houseguests, invariably male and invariably more than one, and so she would wander off. The folly would be her fairy castle or her little cottage, or whatever she wanted.

Sometimes she would be a fairy or a princess, but sometimes she would be a peasant girl. Anything but Lady Grishelda May van Hoffen. It was a magical place, she always thought. Things would appear, and she often wondered if the wood fairies used it as a home when she was not around. Blankets would show up out of nowhere, food, dishes, clothing. . . .

Of course now it occurred to her to wonder if her mother used the folly as a place for intimate trysts with some of her unsavory lovers, but May did not want to sully her childhood memories by dwelling on that. She gazed at her old childhood friend, her folly.

She let go of Cassie, who would stay close by, and strolled around, gazing at the old stone structure.

It was octagonal, constructed of smooth gray granite sometime early in the last century. No one knew why it had been built so far from Lark House when most follies were built to be admired, at the top of a hill or near an ornamental lake. But this one was buried in a planned glade of alder and beech, tall, slim trees that let a dappling of sunshine through their leaves even in midsummer. It was constructed with an open doorway and high, Gothic arched windows that started several feet off the ground. The stone was covered in dark moss near the ground, and thickets of ivy had grown up, obscuring the lovely classical shape of the windows. Tumbled masses of old roses bunched and bloomed at its base.

Maybe she would have the delightful old structure repaired and cleaned up, the encroaching ivy torn down, the leaves cleaned out. . . . She stopped in her perusal at the front of the building. The doorway. The stone step that led into the folly . . . it was stained dark, and the stain seemed somehow . . . fresh. New.

She frowned as an odd sensation prickled up her neck. Had some poor animal, wounded by poachers or by a predator, crawled in there to die? She slowly approached, her heart pounding, though surely that was an overreaction! This was the first time she had been out riding alone since she had come back from London and maybe she was still a little nervous. For months she had restricted herself to rides in the park at the front of Lark House, the side that faced the road. At first she had ventured nowhere without an armed groom, convinced that Captain Dempster would come after her and get her, even though he had been tracked to the Continent by Baxter Delafont, Lord Sedgely, Emily's husband. Her fear had abated gradually, but still she had not gone far alone.

But this morning she had awoken with a feeling that her life was her own. She would take it in her hands and live it again, experience everything she had been constrained not to by societal rules, all of the conventions that women were bound by, when men had the freedom to do what they wanted and go where they would. Oh, she knew that men were bound by society's rules, too, but not to the same extent. And their infractions were more likely to be regarded with an indulgent eye.

And so that morning she had awoken from a restless sleep with the knowledge that she was giving in to them all—to Vicar Dougherty and his well-meaning guidance, and to Sir Tolliver Gowan, her nearest neighbor, and his wife, Jenny, the closest thing to a friend she had had before meeting Emily and Celestine. And she was even allowing Dodo to plan her day-to-day life, though sometimes there was a glint in the elderly woman's eyes that unnerved her with its perspicacity.

But that morning she had retrieved her breeches from a hidden spot in her wardrobe, and she had ridden out using a groom's saddle instead of her accursed sidesaddle, and now she was here, and the feeling of meeting life head-on was thrumming through her veins stronger, pulsing powerfully through her body. It was a nervous kind of energy, like she was going to burst at the seams with a new need to face life head-on rather than sidestepping it, as she had for years.

But what did any of this have to do with dark stains

on her folly's step? Shaking herself out of her curious unwillingness to act, she stepped forward, stooped, and touched the stain. It was not wet, but she had the feeling that it had not long been dry. She looked up and tried to gaze into the interior of the folly, but it was dark. The windows were covered in thick vines, like Sleeping Beauty's palace in one of her favorite childhood stories.

Her heart beat even faster. She had never been a coward, though she had begun to think herself one for the way she had allowed her mother to bully her. If there was an animal hurt in her folly, she wanted to know. If it was not too badly hurt, she would take it back for Bill, her head groom, to fix up, as she did when a child. There had always been a cage at the back of the stable holding a vole or a ferret, rabbit, or mouse that she had retrieved in the woods. If the animal was suffering though, and too far gone, she would kill it to put it out of its misery. She had courage enough to see nothing suffer, she hoped.

She wished she had brought a lamp, though who would do such a thing on a bright summer's morning? But the gloom in the folly was almost impenetrable. She peered in.

"Hallo?" she called, feeling more than a little silly as her voice echoed in the thicket.

There was a sound, and she froze on the doorstep. It was a scraping sound! How she wished for a light! She strained her eyes into the darkness. Was that darker area something, over near the wall under one of the ivy-covered windows? What could it be?

There was that sound again, a scraping! And a . . . a moan? It was ghostly, the noise oddly echoing in the stone folly. She picked up a branch that lay across the stone entrance and advanced, creeping into the folly, feeling her way with the toe of her riding boot. The moan again! It almost sounded . . . sounded human!

Her mouth was dry and she could not swallow, and her hand was shaking so badly the dried leaves on the branch she held made a light whispering sound, like the wind in the trees. She was ready to flee if she saw the slightest movement. Her new bravado did not extend to challenging wild beasts or a wounded poacher, if that was what the moaning should turn out to be.

She sidled into the folly and stood with her back to the cool stone wall, letting her eyes become accustomed to the gloom. The dark patch near the window began to take a shape. It was a man! And he lay sleeping against the wall. Sleeping? Dead? No, not dead. He had moaned.

Who was he? What was he doing on her property?

Still, even if he was an injured poacher he would need help or he might die, and she would not have a man's death on her conscience, even if he eventually ended up swinging from the gibbet. Holding the branch up like a club, she inched forward, waiting for any movement that would signal that he was feigning his unconscious state.

Forward, stop; forward more, pause again. Across the eight feet or so of the folly's floor she made her way. Finally, she knelt down beside him, satisfied by his posture and the amount of blood that pooled around the poor man that he was no threat.

Was he still alive, or had she heard his death rattle?

She reached out to touch him, ignoring the auburn curls that fell forward when she bent. He was warm. She put her slim fingers under his scruffy chin and turned his face up to the thin thread of light that had found a path through the ivy. She gazed and took in a breath with a choking gasp.

"Etienne!" she cried, and the sound of her voice penetrated the forest.

Two

It was him! He was scruffy and bearded, his clothes were filthy and he was pale under the beard, but she would never mistake the only man she had ever met of whom she wondered, "What would it be like to kiss him?"

Etienne, her savior. Etienne, in her folly, badly injured! Etienne, *alive!* She must get help . . . but no, she could not leave him before she knew the extent of his injuries.

All of these thoughts had only taken a second, and the sound of her scream still echoed as Etienne opened his bleary, bloodshot eyes and pushed himself up against the wall. "Back, *vilain,* I will not let you take me!" he shouted in a hoarse voice. He staggered as he tried to stand, and pulled a pistol from his waistband. He brandished it, but then his eyes drifted closed and he sank to the cold stone floor again, his pistol still clutched in his outstretched hand.

May had stumbled back when Etienne had risen, but she stooped over him again when he slid to the floor in a slump. "Oh, Etienne," she cried, feeling a pricking of tears behind her eyelids, "I thought you were dead! What have they done to you?" She knelt at his side, reached out, and delicately touched his hair, his cheek, his feverish brow.

His eyes opened again, and he gazed up at her. A rich caramel brown with flecks of mahogany and amber, his beautiful eyes were clouded with pain and his cheeks were flushed. But his expression sharpened a little. "It is the little English miss," he whispered.

She nodded, unable to speak. Just minutes before she had been mourning the loss of her gallant *chevalier,* and now here he was alive, in her folly! She stared at him, eagerly gazing her fill, overwhelmed by the joy that coursed through her just to know that he lived! But his boat had gone down in the channel. How had he survived? Where had he been for over six months? She had a hundred questions for him, but he was in no condition to answer any of them until he was fed, cleaned up, and rested.

His eyes were closing again.

"No! Etienne, you must get up. You must stand so you can walk back to my home with me, back to Lark House. Do you understand me?"

"No! I cannot," he moaned.

May sat down on the leaf-covered stone floor and pushed her heavy mane of hair over her shoulder. "Why? Is it because you can't walk? I have my horse outside. Cassie can carry you."

A weary chuckle. "No, my little one. I cannot walk, but there is more, much . . . augh."

He had tried to stand again but his face blanched, and he sank back down. May grabbed his arm, gingerly took his pistol, and set it aside on the flagstone floor. One flex of his finger and the pistol could go off! "Stay put, you fool!" She looked him over, and finally found where all the blood had come from. His breeches were soaked on his right side, the side away from her, from some wound on his hip. She reached across him, her hair dragging across his body, and touched, lightly. She heard his quick intake of air. He was badly hurt. "What happened?" she demanded. "Who did this to you?"

He waved one hand in the air. "I ran into a little . . . a little annoyance."

"A little . . . ! Oh, Etienne. Please, come back to Lark House with me." She slid her arm under his shoulders, trying to get him to rise and go with her. "I need to fix you up properly, fetch a doctor . . ."

"No! No doctors, no home. No one must know where I am. Promise me, little one," he said, clutching her arm, his brown eyes dark with pain and fear, the whites shot with blood-dilated veins. "Promise me you will tell no one where I am. It is worth my life if you do."

She let him go, to rest once more against the wall. "Does this have to do with . . . with the trouble in London? With why you ran away?"

He nodded, his eyes closed again.

May thought furiously. She supposed he was right in more ways than he knew. After all, Etienne had been accused of trying to kill Lord Sedgely, whose legal heir he was until Emily bore her husband a son. Although Emily was even now with child, who knew if it would be the heir Lord Sedgely needed? May did not believe Etienne guilty of the heinous crime, of trying to kill the marquess, but everyone else did. She could not even explain the faith she had in him, for it was based solely on a feeling deep within her bones, surely not a rational basis for judging innocence or guilt. At that very minute, at Lark House, Lord Sedgely's Aunt Dodo was buzzing around doing some of her embroidery, or seeing to the preserving. She didn't think much of her nephew but surely would draw the line at living in the same house with his supposed assassin. And May would never be able to keep his presence a secret from the servants. Once they knew, one might as well tell the whole county. Servants gossiped; it was a fact of life.

She gazed at Etienne's dark head, the chestnut curls much longer than she remembered, and at his beard. It was a growth of some days, perhaps some weeks. Had he been running the whole time, for six long months? How many sheds and barns and follies had he holed up in? And who was he running from? Was it just to elude capture as the attacker of Lord Sedgely? If that was the case, why did he not go to the Continent? In his native land no one would accost him for his supposed crimes, especially since all of the interested parties believed him dead. Somehow, she thought there was much more behind it.

The important thing now was to get him well again, but how could she do that if she could not bring a doctor to see him? Judging from the amount of blood around him—he lay in a pool of it and his breeches were soaked—he had been what . . . stabbed, shot? . . . very shortly before he found refuge in her folly. How long had he been here? And where were his attackers; how did he elude them?

A cold shiver passed through her. He might have died, alone and cold, out here in her folly, if she hadn't come out this morning. She would have found his corpse, or even his skeleton! Was that the feeling she had had this morning, the feeling that everything was going to change? Shaking herself out of her daydream, she realized that he was not out of the proverbial woods yet. He was weak, and his wound could become gangrenous. There was no other alternative but to doctor him herself. She was not entirely without experience. Cassie had been bitten once by a badger, and she had let no one else tend the wound but herself. She didn't suppose it was at all the same, doctoring a horse and doctoring a man, but still . . .

"If I can't take you to see a doctor, then we will just have to make do. I can go back to the house and bring back supplies—food, wine, blankets, medicine. I can make you comfortable, at least, and then we'll see what we can do about that wound."

He nodded wearily, his eyes still closed. "That would be much appreciated, little one."

Little one! How she hated that appellation. He treated her as if she were five and he were ancient, though he was not much older than she. "How . . . what were you hit with? Gun or sword?"

"It is the knife wound, little one. And this time not the jealous husband, not like in Paris that time I . . . ah, well. That story is not fit for your young ears."

"Etienne," she said, through gritted teeth. "I am twenty-three, not ten, and I would appreciate it if you would treat me accordingly."

He opened his eyes at that, looked her over carefully, and a ghost of a smile flickered through his eyes and touched his lips. "So old?"

Blushing, May realized she was most improperly clad in breeches and her long hair was unbound and floating around her shoulders. She must look like a little hoyden to him, a girl nearer thirteen than twenty-three. No *lady* would ever be caught like this! But she tilted her chin up proudly. He was not her keeper. No one was! She was her own woman at last.

"Yes, so old. I do not appreciate being called 'little one' as if you were my grandfather! How old are *you*?"

"I? I am twenty-four . . . no wait, I have turned twenty-five while I have run. How about that? A quarter century."

"Ancient," May said, dryly. She stared at him intently, and her heart joyfully skipped a little beat. Etienne was alive! It was so hard to take in when she had been mourning—yes, that was the right word—mourning his death for six months now.

He opened one eye. "Do you think you might get some of that wine? Soon?" he said, plaintively.

She scrambled to her feet. She was acting shamefully like those silly girls in their first Season whom she had observed with such disdain last spring, all of them mooning about over some handsome young dragoon officer. And she was not like them, not like them at all. "I will bring back supplies within the hour," she said. Worry tugged at her as she stared down at him, so pale and so much in pain. "Will you be all right until then?"

"I have been, so far. I will live on, little one."

She stepped out of the folly.

"Little one?"

She took a deep breath. He was ill. She would not nag him about that damned pet name until he was better. "Yes?" she asked, ducking her head back into the shadowed confines of the folly.

"My horse, my Théron—he is out there somewhere. If I call him, will you unsaddle him please? He will stay close by, but I do not like to think of him burdened when he does not need to be."

Théron; oh, yes, she remembered his magnificent black stallion, seventeen hands tall at least, with sleek, powerful muscles and the stride of a champion. She had admitted when Etienne rescued her that she would not attempt to ride him alone. Would he let her take off his saddle?

She stepped out of the folly. "He's here," she called. Théron was with Cassie, and they were nuzzling each other with interest. The stallion snorted and reared, showing off for the pretty dun mare, so much smaller than him at just fifteen hands. "Men," May muttered, approaching him cautiously.

Etienne had dragged himself up to window height with a groan of pain. He whistled, and Théron became alert.

"My friend," Etienne said, speaking his native tongue, "you will allow this young lady to take from you your saddle, and then you will stay in this wooded area, until we are able to leave, do you hear?"

May understood him, having had a very thorough education in French and Italian, as all young ladies did, but strangely enough the horse seemed to understand, too. He snorted and tossed his head, but sidled over to May.

"Does he understand English, too, or is he purely a French-speaking stallion?"

Etienne chuckled. "He understands some English, I believe. He is a very intelligent beast—more brains than the average Englishman."

"You are a beautiful boy," she murmured, stroking her hand over his smooth flanks. The coal black of his muscular body was dusty, and she said, "I'll bring you a treat, my beauty, and I will bring my currycomb, too. You deserve to be cared for, as I have a feeling your master would not be alive without your speed."

She undid the buckle of his cinch as the stallion tossed his head again and snorted.

"You will spoil him with such tender words," came Etienne's dry voice from the window.

May tossed her hair back and glanced at him over her shoulder as she hoisted his saddle and pulled it off of him. "Nonsense."

"He is not used to attractive young ladies murmuring sweet nothings in his ear. He will be impossible to deal with now, all conceit."

Chuckling, May colored and fell silent. Attractive? Her? Who did he think he was, fooling with such gammon? If she knew anything about herself, it was that she was exceedingly plain . . . skinny, mousy, drab. And she knew Etienne's taste in women ran to the opulent, abundant beauty of women like Emily, Marchioness of Sedgely. He liked voluptuous, older women. Her mother would be more to his taste than she herself! Maisie van Hoffen was just his type, if perhaps a little too flashy.

She lugged the saddle around to the back windowless wall of the folly and pulled some fallen branches and dead leaves over it. She did not want even a poacher to happen by and see a valuable saddle—and it was a lovely one, with tooled leather and silver fittings—just lying on the ground. She circled back around again and met Etienne at the window. His complexion was an alarming gray and she realized she must hurry. She didn't know how long he had been without food or drink, but he was not looking good at all.

"I will return within the hour, I promise," she said, touching his filthy hand tentatively. "I hope you will be all right until then."

"I will survive, little one. I must remember to thank *le bon Dieu* in my prayers that he sent you to aid me. I am most fortunate to be in your *petite maison de la forêt.*"

Patting his hand, she turned and headed toward Cassie, who was again nuzzling the handsome stallion. She stuck her boot into the stirrup and swung herself up on her mare. "Stay here," she said over her shoulder, as Cassie sidled, eager to get going again.

"There is little danger I will go anywhere," Etienne said wryly.

May started off, finding the path that would lead her another way out of the forest on the Lark House side, opposite from where she had entered the copse.

"Shaving supplies!" he shouted. "Bring me a razor," he said, scruffing his fingers through his beard.

"If I can. I doubt it, but I will try," she called out over her shoulder. "I will try to be back within the hour." And then she disappeared into the forest, like a wood nymph, her glorious mane of auburn curls bouncing as she urged Cassie into a canter.

"Merciful God," Etienne whispered, sliding back down against the stone wall, "thank you for sending me a sylvan angel. Please let her be as wise as she is brave, *cette petite courageuse*, and let her trust no one. Anyone could betray me. I know I am atoning for my sins, but if you please, let me atone living, not dead. I have killed no one, after all, so let me not die. There is yet much wine to be drunk, and many widows to be bedded . . . and one brave little one to be thanked. Let me not bring her trouble."

The pain in his side had receded, and that was to be worried about. When something hurt, that meant the flesh was still alive. He looked down at his filthy,

torn clothes and his blood-soaked breeches and
touched his pistol to reassure himself he was still
armed. Thank God he had not used it on the little
one. His eyesight was bleary, and his head pounded
as if he were in the middle of a cavalry raid. He had
not eaten in three days, nor drunk a drop in two. If
the little one had not come along he was going to
drag himself to the nearest stream, but now . . . now
that would not be necessary. He hoped. If she came
back.

She would come back. He could trust her. That
morning, so long ago—was it only six months?—when
he had taken her back to London after her terrible
experience with her mother's foul lover, he had come
to know something of her soul. She was brave. She
was resourceful. And there was a sweetness, an innocence about her . . . bah! He did not deal in inno-
cents. For him was the more experienced, the more
sophisticated woman, worldly, who knew what to expect from him.

Hours of expert lovemaking and appreciation of
her charms, that is what a woman would get from
Etienne Roulant Delafont, and nothing more. But
nothing less either.

Not for him the Lady Mays of the world, the sweet
virginal girls . . . though as she reminded him most
vehemently, she was not a girl. He chuckled, until a
spasm of pain wracked his body.

"Oh, good," he said, to no one in particular.
"Pain."

Then he slipped into unconsciousness and slumped
over sideways.

Three

As always, Lark House looked lovely in the early morning sun. The mellow rosy brick glowed, gilded by the rising golden sun. May approached from the back, where a terrace lined the manse, and rode directly into the enormous stables on the east side, the big double doors open as her head stableman, Bill Connors, and his staff mucked out the stalls and prepared for the day's work.

A young boy, a new stable hand Bill had hired, ran to take May's reins. She leaped from Cassie's back and gave her mare a pat on her flanks.

"I'll be taking her out again in about an hour. See that she is curried and has a good breakfast. But not too much." May smiled at the boy, trying to remember his name. "Zachary! That is your name, is it not?"

"Aye, milady," the child said, his blue eyes huge at the thought that the grand lady of the house would remember his name.

She smiled down at him and tousled his hair, extraordinarily pleased with the day and everything in her life.

"You look like a cat whot's found the key to the creamery," Bill said, as young Zach led Cassie away.

Bill had known her since she was a child, and she never could hide anything from him. "Who could not be joyous on such a glorious day," she cried, waving her hands to indicate the brilliant blue sky and freshening breeze outside the gloomy depths of the stable. She tossed back her hair and breathed deeply, inhaling the scent of horse and leather and the curiously comforting smell of manure.

The old man narrowed his eyes. "Peaks and valleys," he said enigmatically. "Peaks and valleys. See you don't slide right down inta th'depths, missy."

"Gloomy old codger," she threw over her shoulder, as she exited the stable. Her breeches had stirred not a bit of comment, she noted, among the men mucking out stalls and pitching fresh straw in for bedding. Bill must have issued a stern warning to his men after he caught sight of her that morning. She could always depend on Bill. He might not always approve of everything she did, but he was loyal and steadfast.

She entered through the kitchen door, a habit her mother had found appalling in her daughter. But Mother did not live here anymore. For the first time May really took that in. Mother did not live here anymore. She, May van Hoffen, was the lady of the house and could do whatever she wanted.

What she wanted was a biscuit. She snatched one from the tray as a kitchen helper took it from the modern oven, and bit into it, rolling her eyes at the exquisite fragrance and flakiness of the treat. "Mrs. Connors, you are a genius!" This was mumbled around a mouthful of biscuit, but the woman, who stood at the low pastry table, rolling out pie dough, looked pleased nonetheless. She was a good twenty years younger than her husband, and as befit any good cook was rotund, with pink cheeks and creamy skin. She ruled the kitchen while her husband ruled the stable, and together they were the heart of Lark House.

"Go on wit you, missy." She laughed. She took the tray from the kitchen maid and set it near one of the windows—they were half below ground, so the windows looked out over grass—to cool.

May laughed and finished the biscuit as she traveled the long hallway from the kitchen to the large dining room and then through to the breakfast room. She entered from the rearmost door, just as Dodo Delafont came in from the grand hall.

"How you sparkle with good health, my dear," Dodo said, gazing at her affectionately. She had cast one questioning glance at the breeches and tumbled hair, but had not said a word, nor even looked censorious. An elderly spinster she might be, but no one could accuse her of being prim and proper, or overly correct. May suspected that it had taken strength of will and a certain amount of independence to remain unmarried as a girl, when she must have been a handsome woman in her youth, and very well dowered.

Smiling, May accepted her cool peck on the cheek, and realized that there would be no escaping. She would have to breakfast with the older lady or invite suspicions. They always had breakfast together, but this morning May was anxious to gather together what she needed to return to Etienne.

"I *feel* healthy," May said. "And happy, and alive! I suppose I should clean up and . . . and do something about my hair, but I am starved. Do you mind?"

Dodo smiled at her and shook her head. "My dear, this is your home. I am your guest, remember?"

"I will not presume upon that to the point of rudeness," May said punctiliously.

Two tall, sturdy footmen entered bearing trays, supervised by the Lark House butler, Stainer, who carried the coffeepot.

"We will serve ourselves," May said, with one raised eyebrow at Dodo. The older lady nodded, her bearing ineffably regal. She looked like a duchess, May had always thought, her white hair piled high on her head, her height emphasized by her rigid bearing and extreme thinness. She had the dark snapping eyes of all the Delafonts, and a tart manner when she was displeased or didn't like someone.

But May had known only kindness from her, since spring when the woman had accompanied a frightened and meek May down to Kent, after the ordeal with the captain. They chatted through breakfast as they ate biscuits and eggs, ham and chutney, talking about the news from Surrey that Dodo had received in her latest letter.

"Emily has been ordered to stay in bed, as you know, and she is not pleased. My nephew will have his hands full keeping her to her promise," Dodo said with a chuckle. She stirred cream into her coffee and laid her spoon aside.

May laughed with her. "No, Emily will not like being confined to bed."

Emily Delafont was seven months into a difficult pregnancy. Her doctor suspected she might bear twins, but she had become anemic and subject to dizzy spells. Emily and her husband, Baxter, the Marquess of Sedgely, had recently reanimated a marriage they both had thought was dead, and the result was she was to bear their child, or children, sometime in December. Dodo, Baxter's aunt, had been Emily's companion through her separation from her husband,

and May suspected she felt a little lost now that the couple were so very much back together.

And so May, even though she had begun to long for some solitude—for no matter how self-sufficient Dodo was, May still felt compelled to ensure that she was not bored to flinders at Lark House, since she had been so kind to her—she could not find it in her heart to even hint that Dodo might like to return to Surrey, and her nephew and niece-in-law. It was going to be even more difficult now with Etienne lying wounded in the folly. He needed her and she wanted to be with him, to care for him. She stopped to consider for a moment how odd it was that she would feel so nurturing toward the man, when she had thought she had no skill or care for nursing, but her mind returned to her dilemma. What could she do? She cast a guilty glance at the older woman sipping coffee—they both preferred coffee to tea or chocolate in the morning—and thought about Etienne, down in the folly, wounded and hungry and thirsty. He was so pale and weak; without proper care he might still die!

"I am thinking," May blurted, "of going out again after breakfast for a very long ride. I have not been over my whole property since coming back to Lark House."

"I thought you already had a rather long ride this morning," Dodo said.

"I did, but I am afraid it only whetted my appetite. In truth I . . . I am quite the hoyden, you see," she stammered, flushing and indicating her breeches and tossing her hair.

Dodo smiled warmly. She placed one of her long, aristocratic hands over May's on the oak table and patted it. "Nonsense, my dear. I have never met a more ladylike young woman. As for the . . . er, the breeches, I have often thought that the reason I never enjoyed riding is the silly way we women are forced to ride. I commend you on your good sense." She gazed at her assessingly. "And the hair is strangely becoming. It . . . it softens you."

Sighing with relief that she was not to be read the riot act for her attire, May said, "I think I will take a picnic lunch with me, as it may take a while to explore all my childhood haunts. I will be riding for hours." She needed to set up her disappearance, as she had no idea how long it would take to make sure Etienne was all right, and to make him comfortable. She felt horribly guilty leaving Dodo to her own devices, but the pull of Etienne, her joy at finding him alive, her desire to spend as much time with as she could, was overpowering.

"Do you . . . will you take a groom with you, my dear?" Dodo asked.

"I . . . I don't know yet. I don't plan to leave my own land, you know," she said.

"So you are feeling . . . safer now?"

Breathing out a deeply held breath, May finally understood what her elderly friend was saying. She was asking if May had finally gotten over her dread of being alone, and her irrational fear of Captain Dempster. "Yes, I feel completely safe." She gazed into the woman's dark eyes. "Thank you for your concern over the last months. I know it took me a long time to come out of that awful darkness I was shrouded in, but your patience and aid have been invaluable to me."

"Enough of that," Dodo said lightly, skirting, as always, any expression of feeling. "If you are going to be gone for most of the day, I shall put my head together with Cook and we shall see what to do about the apple harvest on your lower orchards. The fall festival coming up will be a good time to use some of the harvest, and the vicar was hinting that some of Cook's pies would make most wonderful prizes for the penny-toss."

"That would be good," May said, absently, her mind already turning to supplies for Etienne. She knew in her heart that Dodo had assumed many of the "Lady of the Manor" duties that she should be taking care of, but she had not been able to muster much interest in anything except for the school for the village children, and that she only undertook on the general principle that children must be educated for their own, their family's, and for the country's good. Perhaps she had been self-indulgent this summer, but autumn was soon arriving, and she would pull herself together and start taking care of her people. The school was not to begin until after the harvest festival; she would then devote herself more to her duties. By then Etienne would be well. She would make him well!

She jumped from her chair. "I will apologize for eating and running off, but I am eager to get started. I know I should not have dined in these breeches, but no sense changing when I am off again!"

She strode from the room, Dodo gliding behind her, into the great hall. Stainer entered from the opposite direction at the same moment.

"My ladies, the Reverend Mr. Dougherty and Mrs. Naunce are here. Are you in?"

But the reverend, a good-looking, solid man in his

mid-thirties, strode into the room followed by his
faded sister, Mrs. Isabel Naunce, before May could
deny them. She took in a deep shaky breath of annoyance, as the reverend spotted her, his eyes lighting
up with admiration.

"Lady May! And, Lady Dianne, of course." He
bowed over Dodo's hand, and then took May's. He
looked her up and down, his eyes lingering hotly on
her breeches-clad legs and wild riot of curls. "My
lady," he said, bowing low and kissing her bare hand,
leaving a trace of moisture. "You look radiant!"

May was suddenly aware, as she had not been all
morning, how improperly clad she was. She touched
her hair self-consciously. She caught Mrs. Naunce's
scandalized glance at her tight breeches; the woman's
face was the color of one of her best apples! There
was no way out of it. Unless she was willing to be hope-
lessly rude, she must entertain her guests. But she was
not going to sit in her parlor wearing breeches while
the reverend eyed her!

"I will return momentarily, if you could see to our
guests' comfort?" She glanced at Dodo.

"Certainly, my dear. Run along."

"I am here to discuss the fall festival. . . ."

His voice died out as she raced up the stairs at a
very unladylike gallop, after one look over her shoulder halfway up. She feverishly changed into a gown,
calling her maid Hannah to help, and worried over
Etienne, trying to forget the reverend's indiscreet behavior. Etienne had looked so helpless in his torn
clothing, blood-soaked breeches, and with that
scruffy beard; he was so unlike his usual immaculate
self. But she had found him endearingly defenseless,

and she longed to be back with him. What was wrong with her that she thought of him so?

It was only her gratitude for his former service to her, she thought, that made her worry over him. That, and the normal human care for anyone hurt and in need of aid. Hannah finished fastening the plain gray cambric round gown, and May, impatient to get the visit over so she could hurry to Etienne, only allowed her to coil her hair in the simplest of styles before dashing out to the landing and composing herself to descend in a staid and proper walk.

As she entered, the reverend was speaking, but he broke off immediately to stand and come across the room to bow over her hand once again. He gazed up into her eyes, his own twinkling with hazel light. "I think I preferred you in breeches, my lady," he said, very softly. He winked before turning to guide her across to a seat on a sofa.

May almost could not breathe. So she had *not* imagined his eyes lingering on the lower part of her body. As she had hurried up the stairs she had glanced over her shoulder once, and had found the reverend gazing after her, staring fixedly at her bottom even as he spoke to Dodo. Her heart thudded sickly, and her breathing accelerated. As soon as she could, she pulled her arm from his grip.

She must get a hold of her feelings, she thought, as she felt a welling of panic. She remembered the night she had been kidnapped, and her fear as Captain Dempster advanced on her in the dim room of the cramped cottage he had taken her to, to deflower her for her supposed groom, Lord Saunders. The greedy light in his eyes was the same as the reverend's, she thought, the sick feeling washing over her.

She wondered if, seeing her dressed so improperly in breeches, he had remembered her mother, and the scandalous goings-on at Lark House in the years her mother held court to all her depraved beaus. Did he think her like her mother, maybe? But that was ridiculous! The reverend was a man of God, and would never abuse her like the captain did, nor would he compare her stainless reputation with her mother's debauchery.

And, indeed, when she forced her eyes up from her hands, folded in her lap, he smiled only a normal smile, as he glanced at her. He was speaking of the fall festival.

"Isabel and I would never have intruded at this early hour if we had not felt that we must begin work on the fall harvest festival. Some are talking of a ball, as well, in the assembly rooms, and if we time it right we will have the light of the harvest moon for travelers. What think you, Lady May?"

"I . . . I see the merit of your suggestions, Mr. Dougherty."

Mr. Dougherty and Mrs. Naunce stayed for the better part of an hour as they worked out the details of ball and festival, and came to an agreement on a date six weeks hence. Dodo was invaluable, and gave her suggestions as to a fortune-teller's tent, a penny-pitch game, races for the children, and a grand meal for the whole village and surrounding area.

She was so good at all of this, May thought, watching the older woman easily direct the conversation and plans into appropriate paths. Finally, the reverend and his sister stood as one, on some silent signal between them.

"I fear we have taken up far too much of your

time," the vicar said, bowing yet again over May's hand. He then offered perfunctory obeisance to Dodo. "But I must say I feel we have made an excellent start on the plans. May we return, this day next week shall we say, and compare notes again?"

Dodo, after a swift glance at May's distracted expression, agreed.

"Certainly, sir," she said, graciously. "We will speak with Cook and with Lady May's steward about the harvest before then."

Stainer brought the reverend's hat and Mrs. Naunce's shawl.

Mr. Dougherty paused in the hallway and glanced back at May. "I must give a word of warning to you ladies," he said, his expression serious. "I shall have a word with your steward about this as well, but I thought it best to mention. Warn your staff to lock up securely at night. I would recommend an armed groom patrolling the grounds, too. There have been some minor thefts in the village lately. And two nights ago there were gunshots heard. I fear there is danger afoot. One cannot be too careful."

He bowed, turned, and departed to his waiting carriage.

Four

With trembling hands, May packed a wicker basket with the assembled items she would take out to Etienne. Witch hazel, gauze, ointment—the same ointment she had used on Cassie's leg—laudanum, soap, brush, towels. She rolled two blankets into one sausagelike roll and tied them tightly so they would drape over Cassie's back.

She hauled it all downstairs into the kitchen and opened the basket again. Meat pies, bread, cheese, wine, and apples, some for Etienne and some for Théron. Cook looked at her oddly, but she was hungry, she said, and she would be gone awhile. She buckled the leather strap that closed the basket, and headed out the back kitchen door.

Etienne must be thinking she had deserted him by now, she thought, scurrying across the grass sward that led down to the stables and glancing up at the sun that now ascended high into the sky. It had been three hours! Three long hours since she had said good-bye to him and told him one hour. He would be even weaker, hungrier, even more thirsty!

Almost sobbing in her haste, she lugged the heavy basket and roll of blankets into the stable and called for Zach to bring her Cassie. As she fastened the basket onto the saddle, looping the piece of rope around the blankets, she called out, "Bill, get me one of the mucking out pails, too. I . . . I want to take it in case I want to . . . to water Cassie."

The grizzled man folded his arms over his barrel chest, his forearms knotted with thick muscles. He wandered toward her and said, "An' have ye forgotten the stream, missy? Surely yon stream is good enough for a horse to water out of?"

"No, I haven't forgotten, but I may want to take some water and eat my lunch elsewhere and let Cassie drink. A . . . a picnic, so to speak." She tried hard not to notice the skeptical rise of the old groom's eyebrows.

He shook his head and brought a bucket over, strapping it onto the back of her saddle along with the blankets. He frowned. "Ye're not a'goin' on a trip, are ye?"

"Of course not," she said sharply, as Cassie danced sideways, responding to her mistress's anxiety to be gone. "I am just riding out to the far edge of Lark House property. I'll be gone a few hours, well into the afternoon, I should think."

"All right then, lass," Bill said. He slapped the mare's rump and chuckled when the high-strung animal bolted. No fear. The missy could control a horse better'n most men he knew. But he sure was powerful curious why the mistress needed all that gear. He made his way across the grass up the hill toward the kitchen to speak with his wife.

From the parlor window Dodo watched her young friend ride. Where on earth was May going burdened like that? And with a pail? She had seemed tense and nervous through the vicar's visit, but it could well have been just the man's intent interest in her

breeches-clad bottom that had frightened her. Emily
had told her much about May's abhorrence of men
and of physical contact. With what had happened
to her the spring before it was no wonder, but it was
more likely years of being exposed to the kind of
men her mother dallied with that had caused the
deep-seated fear. Though Dodo was a spinster by
choice, and had little use for the male sex, she could
not help but feel that what May needed was an understanding and gentle man to help her get over it.

But all of that had nothing to do with the mystery
of where the girl was going in such a pother. With her
thin lips pursed in a scowl, Dodo moved off toward
the kitchen for a word with Mrs. Connors. Mrs. C. and
Bill might have noticed something. If anyone knew
what was wrong with May, they did.

Cassie flew the distance on swift hooves. Burdened
as she was, May realized that she had still failed to
bring some things. Shaving implements. How on
earth was she to find that very male necessity without
raising suspicion? And she had meant to bring a cur-
rying comb for the stallion. Next time. It was amazing
when she thought about it, how her life had changed
since that morning. Now she had an object, a *raison
d'être*. Etienne. Gallant, handsome, wounded Etienne.

Of course *she* did not think of him as a handsome
man, not like all the young ladies in London the previous spring. She had seen how they looked at the
young Frenchman, who at that time was going under
the name of Etienne Marchant. And they hadn't even
known at that point that he was the legitimate heir to
the Marquess of Sedgely; if they had he would have

been besieged by matchmaking mamas. No one had known that until he had disappeared, and it was said that he was responsible for several attempts on the marquess's life. May would not believe that though, no matter who said it. She had reason to understand the true gallantry of the man, and would never believe him capable of such terrible actions. Never had she felt as safe as she did with him, for there was an innate gentleness in him that she felt and responded to on some deep level. Maybe he would confide in her, for she had the feeling his trouble went back before his sojourn in London.

Entering the woods, she glanced back over her shoulder to make sure no one from the house was following her or watching her. One could barely see the mansion, atop the long rise that led from the copse to the grassy terrace of Lark House. Even if someone saw her enter the woods, she hoped they would not know her destination.

She slowed her mare to a walk as she made her way through the overhanging tree limbs that obstructed the path. It was clear that no one had ridden this way for years, but it had been kept fairly clear of underbrush, so someone walked the trail occasionally. She pulled Cassie to a halt near the folly and swung down from the saddle. She looped the reins over a low-hanging branch—she didn't want Cassie to wander until the supplies had been unloaded—and walked toward the small structure. She frowned.

It felt deserted, but that was ridiculous. She poked her head into the folly, not wanting to call out in case Etienne was sleeping.

He wasn't there. Where could he be?

Her heart pounding with fear for her friend, she raced around the clearing but could see no sign of him, nor could she see his stallion. She ran to the back but the saddle was still there, concealed in the same mound of branches where she had left it.

"Etienne," she cried. What if someone—who was it he was so afraid of, by the way?—had attacked him and carried him off? He did not even have the strength to stand, much less fight off attackers.

And then an eerie moan drifted on the breeze from somewhere close by.

"Etienne! *Etienne?*" she called, and raced through tangled weeds to the edge of the clearing, and peered into the woods.

The moan again, this time closer.

"Where are you? Etienne, where have you gone?" She heard her own voice, mournful, afraid, and she shook off the terror. She was strong; Etienne had said so when she escaped Dempster. He was there somewhere. The moans had to be him.

She started searching the edge of the woods and another moan took her through some low-lying brush, where she saw a flash of white. It was Etienne's shirt.

"Oh, Etienne, what happened?" she asked, kneeling beside his prone figure.

He rolled over and gazed up at her with bleary eyes. For a moment he didn't say a word, and she feared that he was beyond speech. But then he grinned woozily.

"I thought you went for the constable. I thought you were going to get them to take this wicked Frenchman off your property." His voice was hoarse and dry and he lay limply in the brush, his dirty, torn shirt caught on some brambles.

"How could you think that?" May said, tears thickening her voice. "I would never turn you in, no matter what they say you did. You are safe here, I promise you."

He reached up and touched her face with one filthy hand, his touch gentle despite the grime ground into his skin. She almost couldn't breathe, and she remembered the first time he touched her at a ball; he took her hand and her pulse had pounded as it did now. She had thought it revulsion, but now she was not so sure. His brown eyes were only half open, and he regarded her under his thick fringe of lashes, his smile dying as his tawny eyes traced her features.

"I should have known that, *ma petite sauveteuse*, my little rescuer. I should have known that such as you would never . . . how do you English say . . . 'let me down.'"

"Yes, well, we must get you back to the folly! What on earth were you doing out here? Did you really think I was bringing the constable?" She slid her arm under him, ignoring the prickles of the bramble shrubs and feeling only the warm, muscular form beneath Etienne's shirt. She tried to concentrate on helping him up, but inevitably her hands would relay that despite his recent injuries, he was a man of spectacular physical conditioning.

"Per'aps a little; not the whole way, you understand. But also, I had the business to take care of before you came back, and it was not the kind of thing I could ask your help for."

He was grinning up at her, and she frowned, perplexed, as he staggered to his feet, his weight bearing down on her shoulders. "What do you mean?"

"If I have to explain further, *ma petite*, I will embarrass you frightfully. But I fear I have not completely done up my breeches again."

She glanced down to see that he had missed one button, and she felt her face going a fiery red. Of course! He had to . . . to relieve himself, and wanted to do it before she came back. She didn't say another word as, bowed under his dead weight clinging to her, she tottered up the slight incline through the wooded area, into the clearing.

Of course even the clearing was overgrown with scrubby shrubs, tall weeds, and thick grass. Around the base of the folly, thickets of wild roses tumbled, still blooming even ignored as they were. May supposed she should be grateful that everyone seemed to have forgotten the existence of this secluded little folly. If it had been checked regularly by her steward, or some of the men hired to keep the grounds, Etienne would have been turned over to the authorities, and who knew what would happen to him? He stood accused of trying to kill a peer of the realm, and that was a hanging offense.

A dark vision of Etienne hanging at Tyburn swept through her brain, and May shuddered.

"What is it, little one? Ah, yes, I am not to call you 'little one.' My lady? It has the possessive sound, that, does it not?"

He babbled as she supported him around to the front of the folly. She didn't answer. She didn't want to tell him what she had seen, and how much she feared it was a vision of his future.

"Here we are," she said, as she helped him into the folly.

As he sank down to the floor with a groan, May noticed how very pale he was and how he quivered from the exertion of getting back to safety. It made her frantic, but she knew she must not give in to her fear for him. He needed her strength right now, and he would get every ounce of it.

She made a trip to the stream and trudged back, laden with a pail of sparkling clean water. It bubbled up from a spring on her property, and she had heard that in ancient times it was thought to have healing powers. She hoped that was at least a little true. She unloaded the supplies, and then sank down beside him with the bottle of wine she had brought.

"Good girl," he groaned, reaching out for the bottle. "I am so thirsty!"

"Perhaps you should drink some water first. It will quench your thirst better than wine."

He drew back, scandalized. "Drink water? Water? Water is for horses, not for men."

She drew the cork for him and he took the bottle and held it to his lips, taking a long draft.

"Ah," he said at last, some of the ruby red wine dribbling down into the scruffy beard that covered his chin. "What a lovely burgundy, but what a shame to drink it in such circumstances." He gazed around him in chagrin at the dirty, cold folly.

"You are lucky to be able to drink at all," she said, bracingly. She would not let him sink into self-pity. He was alive, and until that morning she had thought him submerged in a watery grave.

He cast her an amused glance as he took another swig. "Ah, but you see," he said, wiping his mouth with his grimy sleeve, "this lovely wine should be drunk before a roaring blaze in a stone hearth in some woodland manse. The house would be dark and lonely, except for two souls, naked, on a rug before the fire, with the golden glow of the flames flickering over passion-warmed skin."

The picture was vivid and crisp, and May gasped and primmed her lips. "Etienne, how can you . . ." She looked into his laughing brown eyes. "You are teasing me! How can you do that in your condition? You should be saving your strength."

"Oh, but my little one, it is so good just to see you and gaze upon you, that the temptation to make you blush was . . . irresistible!"

The warmth in his eyes made her blush deepen. "Yes, well, enough of that," she said briskly, getting up. "I have brought food and supplies, and I want to make you comfortable, and then we must . . . must take a look at your wound."

"It . . . it does pain me," he said.

"Maybe we ought to do that first, then," she said, getting the witch hazel and ointment out. She knelt beside him on his right side, where the blood-soaked breeches were rent. "You are going to have to strip off your shirt and pull down your . . . your breeches just a bit."

"Never have I been commanded to undress in quite such a martial tone," he said. He kept his tone light. He knew how afraid she was, this young lady, of men. After her horrible experience in the spring with that cur, Dempster, perhaps that was natural, but he had the feeling it went much deeper than that.

She blushed so adorably, he thought, irrelevantly.

"I have nothing in mind but the cleansing and dressing of your wound," she said through stiff lips.

She turned away to wet a cloth in the pail of spring water and he watched her through half-closed eyes, his pain and the wine making him sleepy. She was so slender and energetic, he thought. And she dressed in men's breeches. She bent over the pail to wring the cloth out and he gazed at her bottom. Slender she might be, but delectably rounded in the right places was Lady May. Did she know how outrageously arousing was a woman in men's clothing? Somehow it took the masculine and made it tantalizingly feminine. How would she look clad only in a man's shirt, lying before the fireplace . . . ah, but he must not think of this little one that way. Indeed, she was not his type at all, but she was more attractive than she knew.

"All right," she said, briskly, wringing out the cloth. "What are you waiting for? Strip down."

He raised his eyebrows and stared at her with amusement.

"I have to have access to your wound," she said impatiently, glaring at him as he grinned.

Oh, but it was pleasant to tease her; she was so easy to disconcert. She knelt by his side and tugged at his shirt, pulling the bottom out of his breeches. The first touch of her slender, long-fingered hands on his skin was surprisingly erotic, considering the circumstances, he reflected. She was not exactly pretty, he thought, watching some curling tendrils of hair fall from her tight bun. But her skin was pale perfection, and her eyes were the blue of the sky after the rain has washed the color from it.

He let her pull the shirt over his head and rested

back against the cold stone, wincing at the chill that had penetrated his body. He knew that he was watching her and thinking of her to ignore the pain that spread in a dull ache through his groin. Even now the infection was taking hold. Even now was his blood becoming poisoned. What kind of chance had led him to her folly and made him crawl in to die? he thought.

She was . . . ah, she was undoing his breeches, and how he wished it were another woman and for another reason. Or perhaps not another woman . . . He glanced down. Her hands were trembling and she was making clumsy work of his buttons. Of course the fabric was stiffened with his own blood, black and stiff now after two days.

She darted a glance up into his eyes, and then another. Her breath was coming faster as one button in particular stuck. He covered her hand and gently helped her undo the button. "Th-thank you," she breathed.

The first touch of the frigid wet cloth on his skin made his whole body jolt with a combination of pain and cold. Her hands, still trembling, worked quickly to wipe away the crust of blood. She was a trooper, was this little one. She was the stuff of the English army wives, intrepid, and braver than one would think. She did not shy away from unpleasant tasks.

She had brought a brown bottle and unstoppered it, then soaked a square of gauze. She held it to the wound and he hissed at the streak of pain that shot through him. But her hands were no longer shaking, he noticed, when the dark mist of pain had cleared from his vision once more. It was he who trembled and she who gave comfort with murmured words of sympathy.

"Oh, Etienne, it is so inflamed! It is positively hot to the touch, and fiery red. What happened? I cannot tell, it is so swollen, but were you shot or is it a sword cut?"

"Neither. It is a knife wound, and fairly deep, I think."

He watched her soak a fresh piece of gauze in the alcohol and clean the area more. It was funny, but now that she was down to the business at hand, she blushed no more, nor did she tremble.

"Why are you not married?"

Her hand jerked and she spilled the alcohol.

"Now look what I've done," she said, not meeting his eyes. She hastily cleaned up the spill, then got out a tin of ointment, smeared some on the wound, and put another patch of clean gauze over it. "You have lost a lot of blood; I think your assailant may have hit a vein. The important thing is to reduce the inflammation and make sure your blood does not become poisoned. This ointment should help that." She cast a mischievous glance up at him. "It's good stuff. I use it on my horses when they hurt themselves." She did his breeches back up again, over the bandaged wound.

And so she would not answer his question, Etienne thought, about marriage. Very well.

"And now we need to clean you up a bit." She retrieved some cloths, and a square bar of soap that smelled of lavender, and scrubbed the bar across the wet cloth. With amusement he watched her approach him, as he lay bare-chested against the wall. She vacillated, she wavered, but then she steeled herself and knelt next to him once more. He watched as she swallowed, and then applied the soapy cloth to his arm first. He allowed her to wash his arms, scrub his hands, and then move up to his shoulders. It seemed she was intent on doing a very thorough job.

He closed his eyes. It felt so very good, now that the cloth was warmed with his own body heat, to feel the fragrant soap and strong, slender hands scrub him clean. She rinsed the cloth, and wiped the soap from his arms and shoulders, tracing with her sensitive fingers the outline of his muscles. He was about to languidly thank her, when he felt the damp, soapy cloth on his chest. He drew in a deep breath and opened his eyes. She froze, and her hands trembled as she met his gaze.

Oh, but this felt good in an entirely different, and not so proper, way. She swallowed, and then started circular motions on his chest, the soap lathering through the mat of hair. Down her strokes circled, down to his stomach following the arrow of hair that pointed down to his breeches, and he felt a stirring in his body, a faint pulse. As weary as he was, his body could not resist the sweet touch of the woman before him.

Her voice quavering just slightly, she said, "So where have you been these last six months? We all thought you dead; it was reported that you were on a channel-crossing boat that went down."

"I was on that ship, and it did go down, but it was not so far off the coast; I was very lucky. Some fishermen found me and took me to shore, and a woman in the village took me in."

"So you . . . so you stayed with her this whole time?"

Her hands lowered, lathering his stomach, and then she twisted to rinse the cloth.

"No, only for a month or so. I am . . . I am wanted by many people, and not in a good way, I fear. And so I moved on so not to endanger the woman."

"Where did you move to?" she asked, wiping with the clean water to remove the fragrant lather.

His stomach muscles tightened under her gentle administration, and he realized that he had better think of anything but her hands if he wanted to remain decent.

"I moved to many places. There are in every village widows who are very lonely and very willing to share their bed. The war killed many Englishmen, leaving behind good women."

He watched in fascination as the fiery red crept up her neck and flooded her cheeks. She was shocked, but he would only ever be honest with her. She deserved that much from him. He had always had a way with women, and Englishwomen were strangely susceptible to a Frenchman, and a young one at that, for his women were usually at least forty. He was not used to the pale perfection of skin, as the little one before him had, nor was he accustomed to a woman who blushed so easily.

Her comment when it came was uttered through stiff lips. "Have you no shame? Will you bed any willing woman?"

Her hands shook like aspen leaves in a storm and he frowned, wondering why she seemed so angry. "No, my little one," he said, and then covered her trembling hands, now down near the edge of his breeches, steadying them even though his own were not perfectly still. "I will not bed just *any* woman. I stay away from the unmarried young ladies, and I do not bed *young* widows. They are most eager for marriage, and I, I am not made to be a husband to anyone."

May had stopped scrubbing him as his hands covered hers. It was Etienne's way of telling her that she did not need to worry about his intentions toward her, she thought, starting her task again, but not meeting his eyes. She should be grateful, she supposed, that he would not attempt to seduce her. Not that she could be seduced, but it made their relationship less complicated if they did not have to worry about his intentions. However, she was indignant for some reason, rather than grateful.

"I am still curious, *ma petite*. Why have you never married?"

She slapped some colder water on his stomach as she rinsed off the final bit of lather, and he winced. "Can't a woman just decide that marriage does not suit her, just like you have?"

"Ah, but as a man I can satisfy my natural urges outside of marriage. A young unmarried woman cannot without becoming notorious or"—he leaned over and patted her flat stomach with one damp, but clean, hand—"or pregnant, with child, however you English say it. I believe you prefer our word, *enceinte.*"

"A lady has no natural urges!" May said, finally looking directly into his tawny eyes.

"She does not?" he asked. He held her gaze for a long moment. They were close, for she had found a fleck of soap she had not cleaned from the *V* at the base of his neck, and she dipped her cloth in water and patted at it.

"No, of course not."

"Really," he said. He put his hand around her neck and pulled her gently to him, then, and touched his lips to hers.

Five

Her head whirled at the touch of soft lips surrounded by bristly beard. He held her gently, but curiously she found her bones and muscles incapable
of making the sharp movement that would take her
away from this kiss. She had closed her eyes and all
that was left was sensation: the taste of burgundy on
his lips, the smell of soap that drifted from his warm
skin, the feel of that skin against her bare hands,
hands that clung to his chest and sensitive fingers that
threaded through the damp hair there and felt the
steady thump-thump-thump of his heart. . . .

She was lost in pure sensation and the memory of
that early morning ride into London, after he had
come to rescue her. She had ridden in front of him,
across the front of his saddle, between his muscular
thighs. Weary from her experience she had fallen
asleep against his chest, cradled in his arms. It was
the safest she had ever felt in her life.

And now, alone with a half-naked man, *embraced* by
him, she felt the same odd inner peace.

His kiss deepened and she felt his tongue probe
the sealed join of their lips, but what did he want?
She had no idea but it seemed natural to open her
mouth just a little. Her body jolted with a wave of
shock when his tongue slipped into her mouth and

started taking advantage of her in a most shameful way. Her body felt heavy and weary and she sank against him. His arms surrounded her, but she felt him stiffen slightly.

His wound! She tore herself from him and sat, blinking, in the dim light of the folly. His lips were twisted in a lazy grin, though there was a faint hint of pain shadowing his eyes.

"And do you still think that young ladies have no natural urges, little one?"

Oh! Odious man! He was taunting her. Her face flaming, she turned from him and started packing away the ointment and gauze, and retrieving the food she had brought. "Of course not. I mean . . ." She realized her answer could mean she did still think that way or that she didn't. "You just . . . j-just caught me off balance, that is all." She turned, meat pie in hand. "And of course I know you mean nothing by it. It was just a . . . just an experiment. I felt nothing, of course." She laid the meat pie beside him on a clean cloth and got out the hunk of cheese and a knife, the apples and the small loaf of fresh baked bread.

"Of course," he said, amusement in his voice.

She knew if she looked at him, his lips would be turned up in a smile. He was impossible! Even wounded, he thought nothing of wielding his abilities to make a woman weak. And she had been weak. If she did not tell *him* the truth, she would be honest with herself. The shock when he dipped into her mouth had been followed by a delicious languor, a floating sensation that had softened her will to reject him. But she must not think like that! It could mean something that she was not prepared to accept.

Etienne hungrily tore into the bread and cheese and consumed the meat pie. May took the pail and emptied the soapy water, then got a bucket of fresh stream water for Etienne if he got thirsty when she was gone. Cassie was contentedly grazing in an open area of the clearing, but Théron was nowhere to be found. Humming a little tune, she tore some of the vines away from one window to let some natural light into the dank interior.

Back inside the folly, May looked around and frowned. Now that there was more light inside she could see better, and she could see that it was a mess! Her natural instincts toward tidiness were offended. There was an old red velvet settee in the corner, on the side of the folly that had no windows, but it had been chewed by animals and was covered in mouse droppings and dead leaves that had blown in through the open windows through the years. A small table at one end of the settee was littered with remnants of burned-down candles that had also been chewed.

She strolled over and picked up a piece of cloth on the floor. An old petticoat. A petticoat? It was dirty and stained after years of sitting in the folly, but it was a delicate garment, not some maid's petticoat. It was trimmed in the finest Brussels lace, like the kind her mother insisted . . .

Her mother. She had often disappeared for hours, in May's youth, with one of her invariably male house guests. She said they were out walking, but always warned May not to follow on pain of having her pony taken away from her. But later, May would always find new things in the folly left by the "wood fairies": candles, dishes, food, clothing, both men's and women's. And she remembered overhearing a maid grumbling once about having to go down to "that place in the woods" to retrieve some article of clothing the mistress had left there.

With the knowledge of adulthood she could now imagine what her promiscuous mother was doing with her male guests in the secluded little folly in the woods, but her mind shied away from that knowledge. She didn't want the sweet memories of her hideaway to be spoiled with images of what her mother might have been doing there, in her daughter's imaginary palace, when she wasn't around.

She thought she had come to terms with and accepted her mother's frailty, but a deep well of anger still bubbled to the surface when she thought of the neglect she had suffered. Until Beaty, her beloved governess, had been hired, Mrs. Connors, then a fresh-faced newly married undercook, had been the most mother she had ever known. Maisie van Hoffen was too busy enjoying the fruits of marrying an old man who then had the good sense to leave her a wealthy widow.

As she got older and began to understand more, it was a relief to go off to the Maxwell School for Young Ladies of Quality. Miss Parsons, the headmistress, was rigid and upright, and she gave the young May, bewildered by recent events in her life, something clean and wholesome to cling to. She missed Beaty though. Her governess was more like a sister to her than just an instructor, but after that one dreadful day, and the discoveries she had made about her friend and teacher . . .

May hastily turned away from that memory as from something unclean and unwholesome. She looked up and found Etienne had finished his repast and was watching her. She glanced down at her hands and realized that she had picked up the petticoat and had shredded it into long strips. How strange!

"How long do you think to stay here?" she asked.

He shrugged. "Until they find me and kill me or until I am better, whichever comes first. Unless you want me to leave."

"Etienne!" She felt her heart clench at his words, and a sick feeling threaded through her. She dropped the shredded petticoat and knelt by his side. "Who is 'they'? And why do they want to kill you?"

He shook his head and closed his eyes for a moment. "It is much better if you do not know, little one."

"Augh! I wish you would not call me that! I am not five, I am three-and-twenty, a woman." She sat back on her booted heels.

His look was long and lingering, from beneath his dark and full lashes. "Ah, but do you know that? Do you really know you are a woman and not a little girl?"

She narrowed her eyes and glared at him. If she understood him right, he was impugning her womanhood simply because she denied experiencing base lust. "I am a woman, but I am also a lady."

"That does not mean you must live without passion, little . . . my lady."

"Just May," she said, absently. What did he mean? Passion was something women of the lower classes felt, not ladies. A lady was refined, cool, and lacking any knowledge of the earthier emotions. Passion was a low, dirty feeling . . . just look at her mother, an unrestrainedly passionate woman, loose, wild, with the morals of an alley cat.

But then she remembered something told her by

Lady Emily. No one could deny that Emily was a true lady down to her toes. But she claimed that sexual intercourse—lovemaking as she preferred to call it—with a man, with a husband, was beautiful . . . sacred, she had called it, of all things. The most profane of all activities, sacred?

But she would rather have died on the spot than mention Emily Delafont's name before Etienne. He had wanted Emily, wanted her badly, in his bed. She had been separated from her husband at that moment, and had quite likely considered taking the passionate Frenchman as a lover. And so May would never mention her name to Etienne. She did not want to see the longing in his eyes, the pain of her rejection, and possibly, though he denied it, his love for the woman.

"How wrong you are," she said, rising. "How very wrong. A lady neither feels nor displays passion. All men are subject to it—it is their way—but among women only whores and trollops feel such a thing, which is why men of the *ton* feel obliged to take mistresses and consort with chambermaids." Her conscience nagged her. It was not true, not according to Emily, but she stamped back that niggling doubt fiercely.

He had a half smile on his face, but his brows were drawn down as if he were frowning. "How . . . puritanical. If that is so, then why is it that many of the women these men bed are ladies of the *ton*, unhappy wives and lonely widows?"

"Those women are not looking for passion, but merely for companionship."

He stared at her, his eyes wide with disbelief. "And you believe this?"

"I do! I know it to be true!"

"That is . . . what is that expressive English word . . . ? Fustian! That is utmost fustian. Ladies feel passion just as much as women of the lower classes, and some even as much as men! I think you are confusing passion with something else."

"I am not," she said loudly, planting her fists on her hips. "I know what I am talking about. Maybe you have just never met a true lady!"

He gave a shout of laughter and then groaned, holding his side.

May watched him with concern. Then she shook her head and strode outside. She brought in the roll of blankets and made him a pallet with quick, nervous hands. "I . . . I have to go. I will leave you the food left over and the bucket of water to drink from or wash with . . . whatever you need. I will return tomorrow at dawn. Will you be . . ." Her voice became hesitant. "Will you be all right until then, Etienne?"

He chuckled and gazed up at her with his warm dark eyes. He picked up the half-empty bottle of burgundy and waved it around. "I will be fine and warm, little . . . Lady May. I have this to warm me. She is not as good as a full-bodied woman, but it will have to do for now, until I can summon the strength to crawl into the bed of another unlady-like widow!"

She stood and turned on her boot heel and stalked away. "You are incorrigible!"

She was out of the folly when she heard his voice drift out to her, with laughter in its warm tones. "Shaving implements! Bring me shaving implements, little one!"

Six

Late in the night with the empty bottle of burgundy discarded beside him and his pistol again securely tucked in his waistband, Etienne thought back to the kiss.

The kiss.

Her first, perhaps? She had been unresisting, but curiously . . . He searched for the precise thought, the exact analogy. She was like a tightly budded rose refusing to bloom even when bathed in the soft summer sun, for fear of what would follow—for fear of blooming, only to be shattered by the bold wind or destroyed by a storm. She had tasted sweet and smelled delicious, but her lips were a tight seal and she was absolutely still. Would the bud stay so tightly furled, velvet petals pulled close around the rich red heart? Would she become desiccated as she aged like certain spinsters he had seen, wizening and drying like the heads of the little apple dolls his ancient nurse used to make?

Or would someone take the time and care to pull back every soft petal to find her woman's heart? He rather thought he had made a start. She was not cold, that little one, no matter what she thought. Once he had teased her into opening to him, letting him surge into her mouth, he had felt her body tremble even though she still stayed quiet in his arms. And when he had released her, her color was high, the bloom on her cheeks a rose shade of exquisite hue.

A good husband would go a long way toward curing the little one's fright of men and fear of her own passionate feelings. The promiscuity of the mother had created in the daughter a horror of sensuality, he rather thought. *Quel dommage!*

Etienne squirmed down on the bed of soft blankets May had brought him, and breathed in the delicious scent of lavender that clung to them from their storage place. She had a good heart, a compassionate heart, did Lady May. And a delectably rounded bottom, he remembered, feeling a pulse of liquid heat throb through his body.

Ah, but he must not let himself think that way about her. It would be enough if he helped her realize that there was nothing wrong with a woman feeling passion. That would be his quest to pay back, in an odd way, that which she gave him, as if one could repay one who had given life, as she had.

For he did not mislead himself. His very blood was beginning to be poisoned, and he surely would have died if she had not come to his rescue. Even now his groin throbbed, and he had to hope they had been in time with the alcohol and ointment. He had been in many barns and many stables along the Kent coast and around Dover in the months he had been running from his pursuers. Not always had he been able to find a warm widow to bed down with. It was fortunate that now, on the point of death, he had found May's land, her folly.

He curled up on his side as he listened to the night noises around him, the sound of insects and small night animals moving through the brush. Just days ago he had been living in the home of a very sweet woman, a loving woman, and had begun to feel secure. Now he was living like a fugitive . . . as he was. God had a way of humbling a man who took too much for granted.

He sent up a prayer to *le bon Dieu* that Théron would be all right and would not stray too far. He did not fear someone taking him. He pitied the man who tried to take his stallion, for the horse was not so much Etienne's possession as his companion by choice. No one could hold that magnificent animal if he chose to not be taken. No, his fear was that Théron would be noticed, and that he would inadvertently lead searchers to Etienne's hiding spot. For if the bastards found him now, they could do him in. He had felt himself at the edge of death, staring it in the face, but May, sweet May, had brought him back.

His eyes grew heavy with sleep, encouraged by the last of the bottle of burgundy. As he drifted into slumber he remembered to give up a prayer of thanks for the little one, for her compassion and her courage. A smile curved his lips and he fell asleep with the memory of her lips pressed to his own.

May ascended the long curved staircase toward her bedchamber in the same state of distraction that had made her a poor companion to Dodo all evening. She had lost badly at piquet, a game she was proficient in, and had more than once needed to ask the older woman to repeat something she had said. She explained away her distraction by saying she was tired from the unaccustomed exertion of her riding that day. Dodo had nodded, but her eyes were thoughtful and so May had excused herself and was on her way to bed. She wanted to be up and gone by first light.

She had not been able to rid herself of the memory of Etienne's kiss. Hannah undressed her, brushed out her long hair, and tucked her into bed, but May did not say a word other than "Good night." Alone, at last, the full force of the memory washed over her.

His beard had been scratchy and he had not bathed for days, so the full musky scent of the man had hit her. And yet rather than finding it revolting it had excited her, for some bizarre reason. She had breathed in the scent of Etienne, breathed in his essence, it almost seemed to her, as he had taken her lips in a possessive kiss.

And then he had touched her with his tongue, pushing through her sealed lips with one swift, demanding stroke that had shocked her to the core and yet thrilled her deeply. She had felt herself begin to tremble and had not been able to stop. She was suddenly aware of every inch of his body that touched hers.

In the darkness she shivered and turned over, burrowing under the covers, the cool linen of her sheets becoming warm from her flaming cheeks. Did she most long for morning or fear it? She wanted to see him again, but that was only out of concern for his well-being, was it not? She wanted to know if he was sleeping well, or if he tossed and turned like she did.

She had not had so much trouble sleeping for years. Not since . . . not since the trouble with Beaty.

Beaty was Miss Beatrice Moreland, her governess from the time she was seven or eight until she was fourteen. Beaty couldn't have been more than twenty-one or twenty-two when she first came to Lark House, but she stood in the stead of the mother Maisie van Hoffen could never be to her little girl. Beaty was warm and affectionate, good-natured and intelligent.

Beaty had changed her life with her loving guidance. They had spent mornings in the schoolroom, but afternoons they would ride and talk, read, visit, sew . . . even gossip. Everywhere they went, they went with linked arms and happy expressions.

Until that fateful day, the day May had discovered that her beloved governess was also a woman, a woman more like May's mother than she ever could have believed. Even now, nine or so years later, the feeling of betrayal lingered.

After that day May had, at her own request, gone away to school. It was easier than facing Beaty with the new knowledge of her friend and governess. It had taken months before she could think of Beatrice without a strange feeling in the pit of her stomach, though she had never stopped missing her. Gradually though, in time, Miss Parsons, the headmistress at the Maxwell School, had helped her grow out of her "inappropriate attachment"—as Miss Parsons termed it—to her former teacher. Miss Parsons was strict, and commanded a sternly moral school. It had given May, who had been confused and frightened by her governess's actions, a wholesome influence and a set of moral principles to cling to, something neither her mother nor her governess had spent too much time on, she realized now. She had pulled May from her depression and set her on the road to maturity guided by moral rectitude, not moral lassitude.

She should have been grateful to Miss Parsons— should have come to love her, perhaps—but she never

could feel more than respect for the vinegary woman.
Love was reserved for her Beaty, the best friend of
her childhood years.

May turned over again to seek elusive sleep, aware
that she was sternly avoiding the image she carried
behind a door in her mind, the image of Beaty
and . . . She squeezed her eyes shut and buried her
face in the pillow. Resolutely she turned her mind to
the village school, and her plans for the course of
instruction there.

Early morning mist lay in the hollows of the meadows and clung to the trees as May galloped across
fallow fields toward the glade and the folly. She almost
thought she would find it had all been a dream and
that Etienne would not be there. Surely it was just a
dream invented by her imagination to soothe the pain
of his death, and now, the next day, she would find
the folly uninhabited.

But still . . . She carried more food, more blankets,
and more supplies with her, as well as a broom from
the stable. Zach, the stable boy, had been sleepy-eyed
as she told him to go back to bed. She would saddle
Cassie herself. He had become used to his mistress's
love for the horses and her multitude of abilities with
them, and so he pulled his cap and said "aye," stum-
bling away to find a pile of hay to rest in. He was so
young. Would he be able to come to her school when
it started in a few weeks? she wondered. She would
insist on it as his employer.

Among the bundle of things she had purloined to
take to Etienne was a set of clothing. She had crept
into the attic when she had awoken some time around

4 A.M., and by the light of a lantern lit from the coals in her bedroom grate—it had become cold enough at night that a fire was welcome—she had rummaged through a trunk of her father's belongings, and a valise that held assorted clothes gentlemen had left at Lark House over the years. It was in that valise that May found a pair of breeches that looked roughly the right size for Etienne, and a couple of shirts.

Her mother had wanted to throw out the late Lord van Hoffen's things, but May had pleaded to keep them, and Maisie had acquiesced with a shrug. It was all she would ever know of her father, besides the stern portrait of him that resided in a little-used music room. Now she was glad she had insisted for quite another reason. She had in her possession something that Etienne would be very glad to see.

There was the wood. She ducked under a branch, then slipped off Cassie and led her through the misty, shadowed glade. It was like the dawn of time, May thought, looking around and breathing deeply of the damp, fresh air. Dew clung to everything, and birds flitted from branch to branch, sending out alarm calls about the intruder in their quiet woodland. Cassie blew out of her nostrils and tossed her head. Did she smell the presence of Théron, her equine admirer? How could Etienne risk his beautiful horse to the vagaries of chance? If anyone found Théron, they would have a valuable commodity, for he was worth hundreds of pounds, perhaps more, both as a riding horse and as a stud.

And there, at last, was the gray stone folly, like a tiny castle floating in the mists of time, arising from a dream of years gone by. May looped Cassie's reins over a branch and crept to the door of the folly. A dusty haze drifted inside the stone building and one shaft of lonely, early morning light had fingered through the trees and mist to beam through a window and rest on the man who slept on a pallet of blankets.

May took in a deep breath. He was so very beautiful. The golden morning sun touched his curls where they tumbled over his high forehead, and she thought this must be what the young Lancelot looked like. A stab of longing shot through her body, making her clench against the hideous desire that coursed through her veins. Though she would never admit it was that. It was something else, some fever she had to rid herself of.

He shifted, moaned, and his eyes opened, gazing disoriented for a moment, and then sharpening when he saw her standing hesitantly at the door.

"Little one," he whispered, hoarsely. "I thought you were a dream."

"Yes, I am here, you slugabed!" She moved briskly into the folly and laid down the small basket of food she carried. She laid out fresh bread and more cheese—a Stilton this time—some grapes, chicken, and half a rabbit pie. Then she brought out a corked crockery jug and two pewter mugs.

"What is this?" he asked, pointing at the jug with a crust of bread he had already started on.

"Good English ale," she said, smiling over at him, the picture he made with bread crumbs caught in his beard. She reached over and brushed them away but drew back sharply at the jolt of pure pleasure that coursed through her at the merest touch, even of his bristly whiskers.

"You join me in this homely brew?"

"Of course. There is nothing like good English ale

in the morning, and stout in the afternoon. I will bring you some stout. It strengthens the blood and will help you regain your strength," she said, pouring them each a hearty draft.

"Ah, so I may be gone from your little house all the sooner," he said, with a rueful smile. He picked up the rabbit pie, sniffed it, and then eagerly took a piece to eat.

May felt her heart constrict. "No, Etienne, not at all! Please, do not think I want you gone. You may stay in my folly for as long as you want. I promise you will be unmolested here."

"Thank you, sweetheart." He dusted pastry crumbs from his hands. "Lady May's folly," Etienne mused, washing down his food with a long drink of ale. He wiped the foam from his lips with his sleeve and nodded his satisfaction with the cleansing brew. "You, little one," he said, pointing a chicken leg at her, "have no folly, I am convinced. You are perfect in every way."

Now, was that a compliment or an insult? She shook her head and watched him eat as she drew her legs up to sit cross-legged on the edge of his blanket. Taking a drink of her own ale and licking the flecks of foam from her lips with the tip of her tongue, she cocked her head and smiled at him, glad that he seemed a little more chipper this morning than he had the previous morning. "I think you prefer your women with a fair bit of folly in them," she said, with a grin.

"Ah, so wise is the little one," he said, and winked at her. "*My* women, yes; I think a little folly is a good thing. But you, you are my saint. You are perfection."

It occurred to her briefly that to be a saint was a

very cold calling. But then she bounced up, setting her pewter mug aside. "I brought you something," she said. "Just a minute." She raced outside and brought back the bundle Cassie still patiently bore.

She undid the sheet that held the items and they tumbled across the floor. "Clothes," she said, nudging the breeches and shirts toward him with the toe of her boot. "And look! A razor, a strop . . . even a cake of shaving soap and a brush! And more witch hazel alcohol, because I spilled so much yesterday."

"Bless you!" He scrubbed his fingers through his beard. "I hate the face hair, detest it, in fact. But where did you get these things, the razor, the soap, and brush?"

"They . . . they were left among my father's things."

He frowned at her tentative tone. "Was he a good father, little one?"

"I don't know," she said, frankly. "I don't even remember him. He died before my second birthday."

"Pauvre petite."

She lifted her chin. "I have done just fine without a father."

"Truly, you have done admirably. But I am of the opinion that a girl should have a father. It gives her her first experience of what to expect from men. If her father is a good father, she will learn that she deserves to be treated with respect and admiration." He smiled wryly at his long speech.

"I can't believe you have even thought on such a subject!" May said, kneeling beside him. "You don't want to get married, so you don't plan to have children. How did this even enter your mind?"

He shrugged. "If I did have children, I would like

to have a saucy little girl, someone like you." He reached out and chucked her under the chin, then laughed quietly at her expression of offended dignity. He held up the razor. "I look forward to this," he said.

May eyed him with concern. It was clear that he was feeling stronger than he had the day before, but the razor shook in his hand. He saw it, too, and set the razor down with a sad look.

He shrugged. "It looks like I will have to wait to feel clean," he said. "I would likely cut my own throat if I tried to shave myself." He glanced up at her. "Unless . . . bah, no, I have asked too much already."

"What is it? What can I do?" Just seeing him awake and alive was so good, she would have done anything for him, even take his teasing. He had saved her life once, and she always repaid her debts.

"Would you . . . would you shave me, little one?"

His brown eyes held such a look of hope that it actually hurt to say no, but what could she do? "I . . . I've never done anything like that before. I wouldn't know where to start."

"I could explain," he said. "It is not so difficult, after all." He sat up on the blanket. "Please? I should not ask, but it would make me feel so good!"

His words were almost seductive. It was in her power to make him feel good, and she knew she would say yes.

The water was cold, and the soap was a dried-up little cake, so it did not lather quite as well as it should, but soon she was approaching his lathered chin with the razor, which he had shown her how to strop to sharpness. Her hand was shaking as much as his would be, surely, she thought, but he could not do it for himself without a mirror, and she had neglected to bring that necessary item.

And so she brought up the razor and scraped at his cheek. He stayed steady, his face turned trustingly for her. It took a few minutes but soon she found the rhythm, and exactly how hard to pull to remove whiskers and not skin. Her hands settled as she focused on the task at hand, and finally she was wiping the last flecks of soap from his face.

"I did it," she breathed, rinsing and discarding the razor and gazing at his clean face as if it were a rather tricky painting she had executed. The handsome, clean-shaven Etienne she knew had emerged from the forest of facial hair.

He turned toward her, and her heart leapt at the genuine smile of deep appreciation on his face. "Thank you, little . . . Lady May."

Before she recognized his intentions, he had encircled her in his arms and pulled her to him for another kiss. He smelled so good, of soap and clean water, and she gave herself up to his embrace without a murmur of demure, even though the night before she swore she would not allow him such freedom again. One kiss became two, and somehow she was resting against his body, stretched out with him on his blanket in his arms. His lips had been warm and soft again, and without the scratchy whiskers to distract she became lost in a hazy, spinning world of sweet languor.

He plundered her mouth and taught her, without words, to give back as good as she got. Tentatively at first, and then with more urgent need she thrust into his mouth, her tongue dueling with his in a mating dance of fierce and primitive origin. He pulled away at one point, but she clutched his torn shirt and pulled him back. After a grunt of surprise, he rolled her onto her back and took her mouth in a fiery, questing kiss of desperate desire.

She was lying on her back. *Under* him! Conscious of this at last, emerging from a cloud of passion, she was shocked and horrified by the wantonness of her reaction. She pulled away and scrambled to her feet.

He lay back, panting and grinning up at her. "My lady, you are like the sweetest of chocolate truffles—a brittle crust of chocolate on the outside, still very good, but then, when one bites in, it is to velvety sweetness so good it makes you moan aloud. The pleasure is unexpected and completely overwhelming."

"I . . . I . . ." There were no words with which to counter his shockingly evocative praise, if praise it was. She could not, *must* not, allow him that kind of freedom again. Allow him? She had demanded, begged for his embrace! Shamelessly! Wantonly! She dimly remembered him pulling away and how she had grasped his shirt and pulled him to her again; how humiliating!

Never again. She felt her cheeks flame. What must he think of her? What could she think of herself? And after all these years of self-control, she thought she had overcome . . .

But she would not think of that, of the fantasies and cravings that had plagued her in the years after what she had seen of Beaty and her paramour, until Miss Parsons' strict morality had allowed her to erase from her mind the inappropriate desires she had been prey to.

And there was her reputation to think of, too. She could only do her work, the work of educating the children of the village, if her reputation remained spotless. Parents would understandably look askance at a young lady with those kind of desires and fantasies. If she were disgraced, she could expect no more help from the rector, nor from the draper, the tavern keeper, the doctor . . . all the influential parents of the village. And so she must quash these feelings, but more importantly she must not disappear alone for such long periods of time. People would gossip. Even her own servants. People would begin to wonder if she was another Maisie, slipping off to meet men, as her mother had done. She could not afford that.

She knelt by Etienne and wordlessly redressed his wound, and then hastily gave him the clothes she had brought, turning her back as he pulled a clean, un-ripped shirt over his head.

"I must go," she said, and slipped out of the folly.

Etienne watched her go, a frown furrowing his brow. Then he slowly, painfully stripped off the bloody and torn breeches, exhausted to the core by the time he had them off. She had not even said good-bye. Nor had she told him when she would be back. It left him with a lonely sadness, to think that he had kissed her into a panic. He sighed and settled himself down to sleep on the blankets again, as the morning sun rose and cast shadows, where it peered through the one open window and infiltrated the heavy shroud of clinging vines on the others.

Seven

Etienne need not have worried. May faithfully visited him every day and stayed as long as she could, bringing food and books, a lantern, and the all-important mirror. His hands steadied gradually and he shaved himself daily. She had set about making the small building more habitable and had even, one day, managed to have some of her servants bring down some furnishings, having told them that she wanted to use the folly as a retreat for herself. Etienne lay in the woods a ways off with his bundle of clothes and shaving things, and watched and listened as May directed the men who brought a couch—she thought a bed would cause comment of a most unwelcome kind—a chair, and a small table. They stayed a few more minutes and tore the vines away from the other windows, and then took away the other broken-down furniture.

He was touched beyond belief. Never in his life—since his mother died, anyway—had any woman done so much for him. It humbled him, and yet he recognized that she felt she owed him a debt of gratitude for taking her away from her would-be rapist that morning the spring before. Personally he believed the intrepid miss would have disabled Dempster somehow, and he was sure she would have found her own way back to London, but he had been so glad to be of aid to her, at first for Emily's sake—he had been a little obsessed, he admitted to himself, with the sweet, abundant Emily—but now it was all for May's sake.

The days were getting shorter as September became October, and the leaves turned to gold and began to flutter to the ground around the folly. Night came early and was cool, but he was grateful for the comforts with which she had provided him, though he longed for the one thing he could not have, a fire. He had tried to think of a way, but smoke in the woods would inevitably bring someone to investigate. And so he must make do with extra blankets at night, and cold food always.

He began to think that he must not trespass on her kindness too long, though, for he did not want to bring her trouble. But he did not know where he would go.

Until that time, however, the time when he would have to leave, he would enjoy getting to know the intriguing Lady May. He watched her, sometimes, when she was not aware. She would read aloud to him as he lay on his couch, and by turning his head just slightly he could watch the sweet naturalness of her, as she curled up in the chair, still wearing breeches, smiling over something she read. Never had he been attracted by the slim, boyish kind of woman, but May . . . He could readily see how a man could become entranced by her, her unstudied grace, her joyous laughter.

But as his interest in her grew, it seemed she kept more physical distance between them. When their eyes met, she would always look away, and there was no repeat of that so-hungry kiss they had shared. The

only time she touched him now was when she redressed the wound, and she insisted on doing that
herself.

It wasn't looking good. Even he could see that, for
it was oozing an ugly-looking gray substance and refused to heal, and her brow was puckered each day
as she cleaned it away and reapplied the ointment.
She again broached the subject of the doctor, suggest-
ing that she could swear him to secrecy, make up some
tale, but Etienne fiercely negated any talk of that. He
knew how it would be and he was not afraid for himself, but for her. With a mother like hers even the
most saintly of men would jump to conclusions when
he found that she was hiding a man in her folly. She
would be ruined, and he found that he cared far too
much for her, even aside from the instinctive chivalry
with which he treated all women. He would die before
he would see her harmed, even in so ephemeral a
thing as the reputation.

He could walk on the leg now, but it ached abomi-
nably, and the pain throbbed through his veins. He
stayed off it as much as possible, watching with half-
closed eyes as May busied herself around the folly,
sweeping and washing dishes like a little girl playing
at being a housewife.

But she was not a little girl. In London she had
been slender to the point of emaciation, but country
air, good food, and the increasing security she seemed
to feel was rounding her figure—not to plumpness;
she would always be thin—but she was sweetly
rounded in all the places a woman should have
curves, and he like to watch her natural grace as she
moved about the folly, preparing their lunch or tidy-
ing up.

It had been two weeks and two days. With a self-deprecating grin she told him that she had been forced into the charity she should have already thought of by her cook's curiosity. Mrs. Connors, the supplier of delicious rabbit pie and fresh bread, had become alarmed at the amount of food that was missing from the kitchen every morning. She had accused the potboy of stealing it and May had been forced to confess to her own theft to prevent him from being punished.

But what was she doing with all that food, Mrs. Connors had asked.

"I didn't know what to say!" May said later to Etienne, throwing her legs over the arm of the shabby chair that sat under one of the open windows. "But I remembered a conversation with . . . with a woman who has an estate up north, and she said before she leaves to go anywhere for an extended visit, she makes sure that her cook has standing orders to continue her work of distributing food to those in need. And so I told Mrs. Connors that I was taking food to people." She hung her head, her cheeks blazing with pink. "I am ashamed it took this to make me realize how neglectful of my duties I have been. So I am going out with food to those in need. Even though I don't know who is in need. How do I find that out?"

Etienne laughed. "I would suggest that you speak with the holy man of your village, the vicar."

May blushed even more hotly and squirmed in her chair. "I . . . I suppose. If I have to."

Alerted by her tone, Etienne pushed himself up on the couch and gazed at her. "What is it, little one? You do not like the reverend?"

"He . . . he looks at me strangely. Like he wants to . . . to . . ."

She broke off and looked away, fixing her gaze on the suddenly fascinating leg of the plain wood table. Etienne frowned. Was her exaggerated fear of men getting the worst of her again? He had thought she was becoming more comfortable with herself, but truly nothing had been resolved in her mind. Rather than telling him not to kiss her again, she shied away like a nervous rabbit when he touched her. He could not tell whether it was that old fear reasserting itself, or just the natural modesty of a maiden.

"He wants to . . . what, little one? Kiss you? You are very kissable," he said, gently. "Perhaps you do not know this, but you have many things that a man . . . that a man would find enticing."

"But he saw me in breeches the first morning I found you here, and he looked me up and down and his eyes got . . . hot. And he watched my . . . my bottom as I walked up the stairs to change."

Etienne gave a shout of laughter, though he was surprised that he also felt a spurt of possessive jealousy that another man had seen his little one looking oh, so delectable in breeches. "Perhaps the good vicar should not have revealed himself, little one, but I assure you, it is a common male failing to find such things as a sweetly rounded bottom make one . . . er, hot."

"Really?" She searched his eyes. "If it is just natural, then why does it make my flesh crawl when he looks at me that way?"

He considered her words and then patted the couch beside him. "Come, sit here."

She joined him and he draped his arm over her shoulders.

"Little one—I call you that from affection, not to taunt you—there are two possible reasons your skin crawls when he looks at you that way. You"—he searched for the right words, the words that would not hurt her—"you have some aversion to the male touch, no?"

She shrugged.

"It is natural to be nervous of men, for we are very different creatures from the ladies, but we are nothing to fear. Believe me, any woman who understands her power over us poor fellows has the upper hand, as you English say. Just a look, a word from you, your merest touch can make us your slave.

"But there are men from whom there is much to fear, men like that Captain Dempster, men who delight in giving women pain and humiliation. And so you must understand this flesh crawling. Is it just your fear of a man's desire, or is it because he reminds you of the terrible captain?"

May considered it. "I don't know," she said, slowly. "I think . . . it feels like a little of both."

"Do you feel danger from him?" Etienne said, sharply, feeling his pulse throb. He would kill the next man who hurt her, even if he died in the attempt.

"No!" she said. "No, I don't fear him in that way. I just think his look is too . . . daring."

After she left that day, Etienne lay and thought about May a long time. She was confused, was his little one, and he wanted so badly to help her clarify her feelings toward men and her fears of intimacy. But how could he ever do that? How could he help her? He would have to think of a way, for he did not believe she would ever be truly happy and at ease until she rid herself of these feelings.

May carried her basket into the village. It was her third trip there in as many days, since she had told Cook that she was taking food for that reason. The woman had enthusiastically named names of people she knew could use a little help and May had, awkwardly at first, for she didn't want to offend anyone with ill-placed charity, taken Cook's delectable foodstuffs to some of the needier families. She was starting to get a feel for who could use help, and who would be offended by it.

She spent a half hour with old Mrs. Landon, the former vicar's widow. She was childless and elderly, and Cook's delicate pastries and delicious jams were welcome to her as a rare treat, but May had the feeling that her own visit was almost as important. The people of her village had gotten used to little in the way of largesse from Lark House over the years, but Mrs. Landon seemed to enjoy just talking to May over a cup of weak tea.

Old Mr. Bottril was in his nineties and had outlived his children, even. At one time he had been the head stableman for the former owner of Lark House, before Lord Gerhard van Hoffen bought it in the previous century. Now he subsisted on whatever his grandson, who lived near Margate, could spare from his own family coffers. But May found that the old man was a fascinating fund of information about Lark House and about the stud of her own horse, Cassie. She found herself thinking as they talked and she dispensed a jar of Cook's best beef soup and a loaf of crusty bread, how much the old man would enjoy meeting Etienne and seeing Théron. She sighed. If only!

But she *would* see that Bill visited and mined the old man for information on her mare's stud lines. Her stableman would enjoy the visit, too, she thought, and together they might begin working on her dream, a line of champion horses from Lark House Stables.

And then there was the Johnson family. Mrs. Johnson was only of an age with May, but she was still bedridden after delivering her fifth child in as many years. Her husband worked ten or twelve hours a day and took on extra work from area farmers when he could get it. Prepared food from Lark House was welcomed by the young mother as the proverbial manna from heaven. The poor woman had no energy for baking, nor for soup making or preserving.

The oldest child was a golden-haired little girl, and she stared at May with her fingers stuck in her mouth. May had stayed far longer than she had intended, helping the little maid, not more than twelve herself, who did everything for the weak Mrs. Johnson, to tidy the place and get the children cleaned up. The woman had almost wept with gratitude, making May horribly uncomfortable and aware that she had neglected these people for far too long. She determined that she would ask Mrs. Connors to send one of their kitchen maids to help the Johnsons temporarily until the mother was back on her feet. It was the most solid help she could think to offer.

The tiny five-year-old, the eldest of the Johnson brood, followed her outside when she left and clung to her legs, making May's gray cambric dress grubby with her jammy fingers. But when she knelt and gazed into the wide eyes she was surprised by the sharp glint of intelligence that lurked in their blue depths. She resolved to come back to this house with whatever books of her own from her earliest years she could track down and give the little girl a few reading lessons in advance of the school opening.

Glancing back at the house as she started home, she watched the little girl squatting in the dirt and drawing pictures with a stick to entertain her younger brother. These were the children of poverty, the children she sought to educate so they would have a life and aspirations above illiterate labor. But beyond that, she felt a curious melting in the region of her heart when she looked at the little girl. She thought of Etienne's words about having a "saucy little girl," a daughter. Somehow she believed that he would be a good father for a girl child to have, the kind of father he spoke of every young girl needing.

And so she had become used to her charitable rounds. It was a brisk October morning. She strolled through the town, having made her deliveries, and thought she would stop in at the vicarage and try to get over her ridiculous aversion to the good Reverend Dougherty. For he must be good. From conversations she had had with the Widow Landon, it was apparent that he and his sister did much to make her comfortable. Their charity extended to other members of their parish as well, who appeared to do rather better than those who professed a faith other than the Church of England. It was natural, though, May supposed, that he would concentrate most of his effort on those who attended his services, seeing them as his rightful flock.

The Johnsons were of the Methodist faith, if they

had any faith at all, and were not visited by the vicar. But May intended her school to be free of any denomination, wanting all from Catholic to Methodist to feel free to send their children. Little Molly Johnson, the eldest of their brood, would definitely have a place.

And so she strolled down the dusty walkway by a sturdy yew hedge that bordered the village green. The day was dry and bright, the blue of the sky accenting the brilliant foliage of the turning trees, and she gazed upon the activity of normal village life with a deep peaceful feeling that had stolen over her in the last week. She could not help but feel that it had something to do with Etienne.

She enjoyed looking after him, as weak and womanly as that made her seem to herself. But she enjoyed just as much the hours spent sitting and talking, laughing over jokes shared, and taking their midday meal together, as they invariably did. Dodo was beginning to look askance at her and the amount of time she spent away from Lark House. She could not tell the elderly woman where she went, and so she claimed just to be riding and walking, enjoying her newfound freedom to the hilt.

She nodded her recognition to the passing draper's assistant, young Paul Johnson, Mrs. Johnson's brother-in-law. She knew by sight most of the people in her small village. Lark House was the premier residence of the area, for her friends, Sir Tolliver Gowan and his wife, Jenny, were several miles north, nearer Ramsgate than Dover.

But then, coming out of the tavern, the Blue Hog, two men strode. One was tall and thin, with a look of some quality about him, but the other was squat and swarthy, and his whole figure and stance suggested repressed violence. She stopped and stared, shivering for some reason, though the day was warm enough. They must be travelers passing through, she thought, for she had never seen them before in her life. And yet they seemed to know their way around, and several of the villagers passing by tipped their hats, a sure sign of recognition.

"I see you are looking over the newcomers to our fair village," a voice said in her ear.

She jumped and whirled. "M-Mr. Dougherty! How nice to see you. I was going to call on you and your sister at the vicarage."

His hazel eyes widened as did his smile. "To what do we owe the honor, my lady? We shall be quite overcome by your condescension, I must say. Isabel was quite taken by you when we visited your home. We missed you day before yesterday. Lady Dianne said you were out riding and had not yet returned when we came again to speak of the fall festival. It is our third visit on that mission and we have only seen you once."

"Hmmm, yes, so sorry to have missed you," May muttered, not really listening to him, her gaze returning to the two men who had turned and were strolling up High Street. "Who are they, Mr. Dougherty? Do you know them?"

"We have passed a few moments in the Blue Hog, and they have stood me a pint or two. Not," he added, hastily, "that I make a habit of frequenting the tavern. But a man of God must go where the people are, and many a conversion has been made over a dram of good whiskey or a pint of ale."

"So who are they?" May asked, impatient with his

rationalization of spending time at the tavern. Did he think she cared if he drank with the common folk? He could not be more wrong, as she did not think of him from one Sunday to the next.

Dougherty clasped his hands behind his back and rocked back on his heels. "They are here, I believe, looking for someone, though they have not said as much. But their questions lead me to the inevitable conclusion that they are trying to bring to justice an escaped murderer. Not to alarm you, Lady May, that such a man is loose in this vicinity. They impress me as able, determined gentlemen. They will find their quarry."

"Etienne!"

It was dark already, with only a sliver of moon to find the way. She had not dared take Cassie from her stall, for Bill would have known and demanded to know where she was riding to so late, but she had not been able to get away earlier. And so she had walked to the folly. As she was not riding she was wearing a gown, her favorite, a soft gold color with a froth of pale lace at the neckline, and had a shawl over her shoulders. By the time she got to the folly, her heart was thudding wildly from the unexpected strangeness of the forest at night.

She crept into the folly and made her way over to the couch where Etienne slept. He was not there!

"*Ma petite*, what are you doing here at this time of night?"

She whirled to see him standing at the door, holding up a lantern. Her heart pounded. The clothes he wore were ones a paramour of her mother's had worn a few years back. She had made another trip up into the attic as the weather cooled, to fetch him some warmer clothes and he now wore a jacket. It fit tight over Etienne's surprisingly broad shoulders. He was beautiful, she thought again, awe making her mouth drop open, though no words were forthcoming. His chestnut curls glinted in the lantern light and the breeches he wore clung lovingly to long sturdy legs, the only wrinkle being where the bandage was at his groin.

And she should most definitely not be noticing such things.

She turned crimson and stood, awkwardly. "I . . . I had to come. I needed to ask you something."

He came in and put the flickering lamp on the table. He looked her over and an odd expression blazed in his warm brown eyes. "How pretty you are in that color!" He reached out and touched her auburn curls, massed on top of her head in careless abandon. "And how strange to see you in anything but breeches! I have become accustomed to your attire, you see. You stun me in such a pretty frock."

Pretty? He thought she was pretty? Nonsense. He was being gallant, something he was expert at. He had been known, in the London circles they both had frequented, to be a man who could be depended upon to be kind to the shyest of new debutantes and the most backward of wallflowers.

"Oh, Etienne, I needed to talk to you," she said, moving instinctively closer to him, wanting to feel his warmth wash over her.

He took her hands in his own and pulled her down on the couch to sit beside him. He kept her cold hands clasped in his own warm ones. "What is it? You are agitated, and cold." He pulled her shawl more closely about her shoulders in a tender gesture. "I would not have *ma petite soeur* become ill."

His little sister? How lowering to find that he considered her thus, though she had told herself he was naught but a brother to her, the brother she had never had.

"Your . . . your sister?"

He looked puzzled for a moment. "Sister? No! No, little one. In my religion, the sisters—the nuns, you know—they do nursing. They take care of the wounded, as you look after me. It meant my little nurse, you see."

She felt an overwhelming relief, and could not for the life of her imagine why it mattered if he had thought of her as a little sister. Did he have a sister? Did he have family? She stored away that question to ask him at another time, but right now she had to tell him.

"Etienne, there were two men in the village. Mr. Dougherty says they told him they are there looking for an escaped murderer. You . . . you are not who they are . . ." Her voice faltered and trailed off.

"What did they look like?" he asked.

He was squeezing her hands rather tightly, she noticed as she described them. He turned pale and fear glazed his eyes. She knew that Etienne was one of the bravest of men, with a foolhardy courage that had taken him through many difficult spots, as he had told her, in describing some of the places he had been in his travels. He recognized her description and he feared them; she was sure of it. If he was afraid, it must be very bad.

He stared into space, and she gazed steadily at him. What was this feeling she had for him? she wondered.

She reached up and tucked one of his dark curls behind his ear, and he grasped her hand, turning her palm to his lips and kissing it. Her insides quivered and she leaned against him, sighing with deep satisfaction when he encircled her in his arms.

The night noises rustled around them, and a breeze through the open Gothic window made the lamp gutter and go out. They were alone in the utter darkness and she found herself burying her face in his neck, breathing in his clean scent, feeling the pulse of his strong heart pushing blood through his veins. She raised her head and found his lips, covering them with her own, the banked fires she had tamped down since their last kiss, blazing into a scorching heat between them.

In the dark there was no right or wrong, and as he lowered her down to the couch and pulled her to him she responded to his ardor, winding her arms around his neck, kneading the muscular swell of his shoulders, allowing her hands to trace the bunched muscles of his back.

He murmured in French, sweet phrases that became nonsense in her befuddled brain as the heat of their shared kisses—wet and warm, tongue touching tongue, eager bodies pressed to each other—sent prickles of excitement over her body. His hands spanned the smallness of her waist and cradled her hips, pulling her against him as he lay beside her, pulling her slender form under his own.

And then his hands wandered to her limbs, and he reached down and pulled her knee up over his leg, bunching her dress up high, until he was cradled between her thighs in the most shamefully wanton way. She gasped into his ear, "Etienne, no!"

He stilled, and she could feel him swallow with difficulty and breathe deeply, trying to control the deep
panting and thudding of his heart. She could feel that
organ thumping against her breast and it caused the
strangest shuddering through her body. She became
aware of every inch of him pressed against her, even
down to an odd ridge in the front of his breeches that
she did not think could possibly be the bandage at
his groin.

"I . . . oh, Etienne!" She pulled away from him and
he released her without hesitation. "I have to go,"
she cried into the darkness and stumbled from the
folly. The moon glinted through the bare branches
lighting her path home, and she ran all the way.

He groaned into the night and doubled over on
the couch. He ached with desire and pushed the heel
of his hand into his groin, trying to stifle the pulsating
need that had him cursing his male body for betraying
him. He had no business touching the innocent
young miss that way and he should be deeply ashamed
of himself.

But instead all he could think about was the way
she fit under him, and how her slender leg had arced
over his, allowing him a most improper access to a
heated warmth that she denied, even as she felt it.
She was ashamed of her passionate nature; he knew
that now, and thought it a pity. No doubt she thought,
by responding to him so eagerly, so sweetly, she was
descending into the licentious depths of her mother,
whose reputation across England and even to the
Continent was that of a whore.

But May was not her mother and someone should
teach her that, that passion was not dirty, and that
some man would be exceedingly lucky to have such

a fine, sweet, compassionate, and yes, passionate woman as his wife. A man would never need more. There was nothing tawdry about her. She was a shining example of budding young womanhood, if only she would recognize it in herself.

But she was not for him. He liked an older woman, with more bounty, the fuller bosom, the rounder stomach . . . and experienced! He was not marriageable, even if he solved his current problems. *Non, mais non.* He was not marriageable, and the little one, she should be married.

He turned over on his stomach and stifled his groan into his pillow.

So why did he ache for her? Why did the sweet curve of her derriere haunt his dreams, and the softness of her skin make him long to touch her, to open her blouse and caress her small breasts?

Mere lust, he determined. He was a man who had not had a woman for too long, given his own passionate nature. Perhaps it meant his body was recovering apace. That was a thought to cheer one.

But the little one was not for him, no matter how much he wanted her. And he did want her badly; he could not fool himself. And no, it was not just that he had not had a woman for too long, it was her, May. It was her innocence that drove him to distraction. He had never been attracted to innocent young ladies—had stayed away from them purposely, in fact—but May was different.

He liked her. He respected her. And he wanted her.

But he could never have her. That right belonged to the man who would claim her in marriage.

He must not think of that man, or he would gnash his teeth in the most degrading way, to think of that stranger who would first touch her nakedness and arouse her to a fevered height, who would first give her the completion of the desire she felt. And so he would think of the news she had brought him.

He had recognized her description immediately—the tall, thin man with the look of Quality. It was Delisle. Delisle was near. He thought he had left enough false trails that they would never track him down, but they were so close. Was he endangering May? Should he leave? He must decide before daybreak brought her to his side again.

Eight

Lady Dodo Delafont squinted down at the letter she was writing to her niece, Emily, then sighed and put on her spectacles. Age! She was getting old, and there was no denying it. She had stopped celebrating birthdays when she was fifty, almost twenty years ago now, but that did not mean that she stopped getting older.

She glanced over at May, who sat in a chair by the window of the small morning parlor they shared. The girl was gazing pensively out over the terrace of Lark House, and down the broad swath of green lawn toward a copse of trees in the distance. Every so often her color would change, and her cheeks would blush a becoming rose, and then she would pale, all while she picked at her shawl fringe.

Dodo would have given much to know what was causing this unusual blue mood. She had not known May before the spring of that year, and the girl had been through so much turmoil, that who knew what her normal personality was like? But she had felt a kinship with the girl that she thought stemmed from a shared disdain of artifice, a contempt for men, and a vigorous need to keep busy.

And yet lately the girl had demonstrated a secretive side to her character. She had always been private, even reticent, though not especially shy, but Dodo had thought it was just comparable to her own dislike of excessive emotionalism. But suddenly the girl was going out for hours with only a vague indication of where she was going or where she had been, when in the past months she had been completely open about everything. She had outfitted the folly down in the woods with furniture, and Dodo suspected that May spent a good deal of her time there, but doing what?

And that was just one of the mysteries at Lark House. The housekeeper complained to the butler that she thought there were some blankets missing from the linen storage, and some of the housemaids had started talking about ghosts that tread the attic in the small hours of the night. Dodo didn't believe in ghosts. Nor did she believe that blankets could disappear into thin air. But this was not her home; if May was purloining blankets, they were, after all, her own. In any other young lady Dodo would have thought that the sudden secrecy meant she had taken a lover, but that was ridiculous. Emily had told her about the girl's aversion for men.

And May was not a child but a grown woman capable of ordering her own life as she saw fit. She was evidently recovered from the fear that had plagued her after that unfortunate kidnapping incident in the spring. Perhaps it was time to think about going back to Brockwith, where Emily had been ordered to bed late in a very difficult pregnancy. She longed to be with her most beloved niece—niece by marriage only, but more kin to her than anyone on earth—especially in a time when she felt that she could be of help in keeping her amused during long hours spent in bed.

She set the spectacles on her nose and took up her

quill again, dipping it into the ink and continuing the letter to Emily. She rather thought May would be fine without her company, and certainly they spent very few hours of the day together now. She would broach with Emily the subject of leaving and see what she said.

She had not gone to him that morning. She had not been able to face him after throwing herself at him so shamelessly the previous night. What must he be thinking? Likely what she thought of herself, that she must be the worst wanton in England, besides her mother. May stared disconsolately into the distance, to the misty copse of trees that held the folly deep in its woody depths, and Etienne.

She had lain with him like a trollop, pressing herself to his powerful body as though she wanted to be taken, kissing him with abandon. But the thought of those men after him . . . Oh, it had been too much! She cared more for him than she wanted to think, and could not bear the thought of someone taking him away to hang at Tyburn.

But who was this who was after him? Was it for the supposed attempts on Lord Sedgely's life? Surely, as he was innocent, there was nothing they could do to him?

Or were these men after him for something else?

Stainer came to the door of the morning parlor and bowed low. "Reverend Dougherty to see the ladies," he said in his sonorous tenor.

The vicar came in smiling and bowed over Dodo's hand, and then crossed the room to May. He took her hand, bowing and holding it much too long. His eyes did a slow crawl over her body, and she repressed the shiver she always felt in his presence. Had he never learned how a gentleman treated a lady? Etienne, for all his teasing attentions and suggestive remarks, never made her feel like she was naked and vulnerable.

"My lady, you are looking especially fine this morning! Autumn colors become you as no other."

Her chin shot up, as it always did when she suspected insincere flattery. She compared his obsequious words with the warm admiration in Etienne's eyes, and it made her realize that her friend had meant what he said the previous night, when he told her she looked pretty. Now she could see the difference between empty flattery and the truth. It made her heart thud to know that Etienne had genuinely found her attractive.

"What brings you here this morning, Mr. Dougherty?" She sat down in her chair, and indicated the sofa.

Dodo joined them. "Yes, Mr. Dougherty. We did not expect to see you until the end of this week, when we have our next meeting about the fall festival."

"Ah well, how can I resist visiting two beautiful ladies on any flimsy excuse?"

Dodo and May exchanged a look of perfect understanding. The butter boat had just been upended over both of them and they were thoroughly soaked.

"And what would that flimsy excuse be?" May asked, dryly.

Dougherty had the grace to look sheepish. "Actually I am here on business for my sister." He turned to Dodo. "My sister reminded me that when last we spoke, you said you would find the knitting pattern for a set of baby's clothing. She was thinking she would make a few items for the ladies' booth.''

"Ah, yes!" Dodo said. "We were speaking of my niece's coming confinement, and the woolens I am making for the baby . . . or babies, for it is possible she will have twins. I told Mrs. Naunce I would copy out the pattern for her, and I have done so. I was going to send a footman down to the vicarage with it if I was not free within the next day or so."

"Well you see before you a 'footman' sent to do his sister's bidding!" Mr. Dougherty cried. "Would you be so good as to retrieve the pattern? She is anxious to start as soon as possible, as the festival is only a little more than four weeks away now. She will need some time to produce a few sets."

Dodo rose and excused herself, and May politely asked the vicar if he cared for tea.

His expression serious, he shook his head. "Actually, my dear Lady May, I have a second purpose for coming today, and I am so glad to have the opportunity to speak to you."

May raised her eyebrows. "And what could that be, sir?"

"Do you remember yesterday when we spoke about the gentlemen coming out of the tavern?"

Her heart thudding, May nodded, not trusting her voice.

"I have since learned more from them. Last evening I accosted them in the tavern's taproom, and we fell to talking. This killer for whom they are searching is a Frenchie, and you know what atrocities they are capable of, murdering bas . . ." He colored. "Pardon my language, my lady. Every Englishman is hardly rational on the subject of those scummy foreigners."

"Surely the reason we fought this last war was as much in support of the French as against them," May said, holding her anger in with difficulty. "After all, more French suffered at the hands of their own people than did English."

"There is much in what you say, of course, but it just goes to prove what a murdering race they are, to be sure, killing their own kind so easily. But that is far afield from what I must say. This Frenchie tried to kill one of the quality in London, and now he is on the run. These gentlemen are Bow Street runners, and they are pledged to bring the filthy animal down. He could be anywhere! They ask for our aid in finding and bringing him to justice."

May's hand went to her neck and her breathing was almost choked off, her fear thickening her throat.

Correctly interpreting her gesture as alarm but misunderstanding the source, Mr. Dougherty became ardent, moving to the edge of his seat and gazing at her with adoration. "My lady, I would lay down my life to protect you! Do not worry, I will do all in my power to find this animal and bring him in."

May hardly heard him. Bow Street runners? Who would have hired them to find Etienne? How could anyone know Etienne was still alive to hunt, for Lord Sedgely himself had discovered that Etienne went down in the channel crossing. He was presumed drowned, and all searching for him was called off. None of it made any sense.

There was more to the story than just the attempts on Lord Sedgely's life, and Etienne had better be prepared to tell her, because she was tired of his evasions. She could not help him if she only knew part of the story.

She was suddenly aware that Mr. Dougherty had clasped her hand in his and was pressing it to his jacket. She gave a tug, but he was not prepared to relinquish his prize before he had his say.

"My lady . . . May, if I might presume to call you that . . ."

"You may not!" May exclaimed.

Disconcerted, he loosened his hold momentarily and May jerked her hand away from him.

"As . . . as I was saying, I would do anything to keep you safe, my lady. And that is why this very minute I have your steward, Mr. Crandall, organizing the stable hands and groundsmen. I intend to lead a search of your land to be sure that you are absolutely . . ."

"You did what?" May said, leaping to her feet.

"I am organizing a search pa . . ."

"On whose authority?" May felt an acid mixture of fear and anger roil through her. Fear won, and she almost could not breathe. Etienne! They would find him, hunt him down like a fox, and hand him over to . . . to those men, whoever they were. She did not for one minute think they were really Bow Street runners, but she still did not know who they were. Etienne did. She had seen that in his eyes the previous night.

And then anger surged to the forefront again and she pointed one shaking finger at the reverend. "How dare you order my men to do anything? You have no right!" She strode to the corner of the room and jerked the bellpull. Stainer was there instantly. "Tell Mr. Crandall that he is to cease this minute whatever he is doing. I wish to see him immediately—in the library, Stainer."

The butler bowed and exited and May looked up to find that the reverend had crossed the room and

stood near her. Calming her erratic breathing with
an effort, she said in a calmer voice, "Sir, you have
taken too much upon yourself. This is my land, and
I am the only one who may order my men to do anything. I am not convinced of this so-called threat."

"But, my lady," he said, his voice softer and with
an oily sound, "you are a young lady alone, and in
need of a man's protection. My dear, you do not know
the dangers that lie outside your door as a man does.
Let me be the one to guide you, to help you . . ."

"Mr. Dougherty! I am not your 'dear'! You presume
upon our acquaintance. I may be 'merely' a woman,
but I am very capable of taking care of my own land!"

"Ah, of course you are, er, capable, but a lovely
young lady like yourself should only be thinking of
feminine things, the latest fashions and poetry, music,
frivolity. . . . Let a man take care of the business." His
voice was conciliatory, meant to flatter her into acqui-
escence.

Gazing at him in disbelief, she suddenly understood him. He was hoping to insinuate himself into
her good graces. He thought that at her advanced
age, a spinster of all of three-and-twenty, she was on
the hunt for a husband. He had the temerity to think
that he could make himself indispensable, after which
he would no doubt spout some foolishness about having fallen in love with her and ask for her hand!

Fortune hunter!

It was not the first time nor would it be the last that
she would find herself the object of someone's attention, only to realize that their motive was her large
inheritance, full control of which she would attain on
her twenty-fifth birthday, or upon marriage.

If there was anything in the dance between men

and women she was good at, it was repulsing the advances of a fortune-hunter. "I am not interested in the latest fashions. I despise poetry. I manage my *own* land. No one takes over from me my duties." She stared directly into his hazel eyes, and saw that he understood her. "And now, sir, if you will excuse me, I have some impertinent orders to countermand, orders that should never have been given."

She stalked from the room, leaving behind the reverend, who watched her go with eyes gone suddenly very cold. He frowned at her retreating figure as suspicions whirled through his brain. What was she more angry at, his presuming to order her men around, or his idea to search her land? It would bear some investigation, he thought.

Nine

Mr. Crandall turned out to be adamant on the point of having the Lark House land searched, and she had to threaten to sack him before he gave in to her order. Perhaps she would sack the old codger anyway, she thought, as she changed from her gown into breeches. Hannah, in stiff-lipped disapproval, provided her with the soft cambric shirt she wore when she went out riding, and she pulled it on over her head and tucked it into the waistband of the breeches, feeling a new snugness in them. It had not escaped her attention that she had gained a stone in weight, and it had made her body rounder, softer than it had been. She stared at herself in the cheval glass as Hannah took her gown and rustled away to the wardrobe to put it away.

Yes, her body had a softer silhouette now, less angular, though she was still slender. She ran her hands down over her hips, and then the memory of Etienne's hands, pulling her body against his leapt into her mind and she turned away from the mirror in confusion, and started out of the room and down the stairs. She must not think of that! It left her feeling hot and strange, as though she didn't even know her own mind anymore.

Crandall. Yes, Crandall. Her steward had proved

stubborn on many fronts. May wanted to take advantage of some of the new theories in agriculture for the home farm and the orchards, but he dismissed them as foolishness. Things had been done the way they were done for fifty years. No reason to change.

She had tried to explain that in reviewing the records, she had noticed that yields had been steadily falling, but he did not even appear to hear her. Her mother had never interfered in his absolute control, and he did not believe any woman could understand agriculture. He would have to go if she wanted to institute any of the myriad changes she had planned for her land.

She rode out on Cassie, needing to rid herself of some of the angry energy she had bottled up in trying to be diplomatic with two men as foolish and stubborn as the reverend and Mr. Crandall. She galloped over the long swath of green, through a fallow pasture and then jumped off Cassie and let her rest.

Well, she had taken care of the present situation. And now there was another matter she must settle one way or another. She strolled through the long yellowing grass and tangled weeds, kicking with her booted foot at clods of earth and small stones. It was a warm-enough day that she did not even need a jacket, and the October sun beat down on her neck with friendly heat.

She walked and thought about the new dilemma in her life. Her mother had written her several letters in the last few weeks. After a resentful silence of some months, Maisie had written that she would like to come and visit her daughter, but she needed her permission because that was the agreement they had signed after that debacle in the spring, a situation that was inadvertently her mother's doing in taking to her bed that horrible, sadistic creature, Captain Dempster.

But her mother now sounded contrite, and May could not help the softening in the region of her heart. Her mother was who she was. She said she had been behaving herself of late, and in fact had not gone back to her old ways after that awful time in the spring. Her daughter would not even know her, she had become so circumspect. Her affair with Dempster had been a kind of madness, one that she bitterly regretted now. That she had risked her daughter's life would always haunt her, and so it should, she wrote.

She wanted to visit her daughter to discuss her future plans, and to assure herself that May was all right.

But how could May believe her? She wanted to, but her mother's past told against her. Her mother had been shockingly immoral, and May blamed her even for her beloved governess's fall from grace all those years ago. After all, it was one of Maisie's guests who was with Beaty. . . .

With a shock, May realized that Beaty was just four years older than May was now when last she had seen her. Had she felt about that man the same way May felt every time she touched Etienne? Did that man's kisses burn into her? Is that what led to . . . Her thoughts shied away from the memory of a day that was burned into her brain, the day she lost some innocence about relations between men and women.

May remounted and rode some more, ending up, inevitably, at the folly. She did not tie Cassie to a branch this time, knowing she would stay in the wooded grove and would not wander far from her. Through the branches May could see Théron, the coal black of his coat a dark shadow in the wood as he moved silently toward the open area around the folly. She smiled, noting that Cassie was moving toward the black stallion as he entered the clearing. They were drawn together, it seemed, even as she felt drawn to Etienne.

She stepped into the folly. Etienne was sleeping on the couch, stretched out, one arm flung over his eyes and the other stretched across the couch. He was deeply asleep, and she gazed at his perfect, lithe body, her heart beating hard and the liquid warmth she had come to recognize beginning again in her loins. Trembling, she lay down beside him, sharing his pillow, cradled in the curve of his outflung arm.

Is this what a woman feels who wants to lie with a man? she wondered. She felt restless and wild inside, and could not stop picturing his hands as they were the night before, roaming over her body, cradling her bottom, lifting her leg over him. And all the while his tongue probing her, searching her, making her squirm with ecstasy. She would have given anything to feel his tongue and lips on her naked skin. . . .

But she must not think that way! It was wrong. She curled up to his body, and his warmth and the quiet comfort of his breathing made her drowsy. How nice it would be to have him with her all the time, every night, to sleep beside like this. He shifted to his side, and her eyes flew open, when she felt him pull her body close.

But he was still asleep. And she had to admit it felt rather nice, him so close, his leg and arm over her in a protective gesture, his body so close . . . so close. . . .

She drifted into sleep, and the midday shadows shifted across the wall of the folly. The sun was able to light up the folly better now, with the leaves of the alders and beech trees falling in little golden drifts on every autumn breeze. It peeked into the small structure and touched the two sleeping figures with a soft gilding and sunny warmth.

Etienne sighed and stretched slightly, awakening to the knowledge that he had been having a wonderfully naughty dream and that he was thoroughly aroused, as he often was now. A soft, slender body was curled into his own and he opened his eyes, startled. May?

Yes, May. She was curled up against him with one arm around his waist, and he was lying almost on top of her, one slender, breeches-clad leg between his and snug against his groin. He pushed against her languidly, nuzzling the fragrant softness of her hair, but then stopped, rigid with shock as his mind fully awakened. Had he blacked out and forgotten doing something, lying with her? But no, that could not be, for he had no head injury, no reason for blackouts.

So she must have come to the folly while he slept and lain down beside him. She had not visited him that morning. After their late night tryst he had feared that he had frightened her away for good. And after that, why did she lie with him now? Had he overcome her fear of men? Was this some sign that she wanted him as he now acknowledged he wanted her?

Or perhaps it was just that she was sleepy.

He propped himself up on one elbow and gazed at her. The sun drifted in through bare branches, and the soft cambric shirt she wore molded to her small, perfect breasts. The fabric was worn and through it he could see the darkening at the tips, and his mouth watered. Every instinct told him to touch her, to caress her, to let her know how desirable she was and that there was nothing to be frightened of in her sensuality. He ached to love her slender body until she cried out in ecstasy.

But no. He must not think that way over this little one.

He gazed instead at her face, soft and strangely childlike in repose. She was not pretty, or at least not in the usual sense that men said a woman was pretty. She had not the blond curls, nor the retroussé nose, nor the perfect small mouth. Her mouth was too large, her features too sharp, and her forehead too high.

Ah, but when she laughed . . . When she laughed her face lit up and her eyes, so pale blue like the sky, they sparkled when she was merry, and he had made her laugh many times just to see that glimmer. She had a sweet nature hidden under a tart manner, and a passionate heart and body hidden by her reserve.

He traced her mouth with the tip of one finger and she pursed her lips. Her mouth opened then and he gave in to the urge to kiss her, covering her lips with his own, deepening the kiss as his arousal pulsed with awareness of her as a desirable woman.

She gave a long, purring "Mmmm" of satisfaction and stretched, kissing him back and languidly flexing her body under his. Like a cat awakening, she rubbed herself sinuously against him. His breathing quickened and his kiss became deeper and wetter, as his hand slid down over her body, memorizing the curves that undulated like the low Kentish hills.

Mon Dieu, but she was sweet, his little one, like

honey dripping from a comb. She turned to him and pressed herself to his body, burrowing her lips into his neck and clinging to his shoulders, her slender fingers digging into the muscles. He held her close, and his hands wandered freely, cupping her bottom, kneading her thighs, and he pushed against her, finding sweet relief in the feminine valley between her legs.

Ah, it had been too long, and she wanted him; he knew it with every particle of his being.

And yet . . .

She was such an innocent. He pulled back from her, groaning when she would urgently rub against him, almost defeating every chivalrous urge for the violent desires of his body. He longed to peel her breeches from her and touch her, bring her to wriggling satisfaction, and then take his own, sinking into her. . . .

Augh! Enough. He was torturing himself to no end, for he would not take advantage of her semiconscious state. Besides, he honored her innocence and would preserve it from his own desire.

"Little one," he whispered, gazing down at her.

"Etienne," she whispered back, in a voice that deserved to echo in a dark bedchamber. It was a soft voice rich with desire, sweet with drowsy passion.

He took her shoulders gently in his hands and shook lightly. "Little one, awaken."

"Etienne, please," she whispered, and then pulled him down for another kiss.

What a delicious dream. She sighed, and licked her lips. And then she felt the warmth of a body next to hers. She opened her eyes to see Etienne's tawny gaze and smiling face close to her.

Oh. Oh my. It was not a dream after all! She had been shamelessly rubbing herself against him like the tramp she never wanted to become, just like her mother! Feeling the heat rise to her cheeks, she stumbled from the couch, her riding boots thudding against the stone floor. Her hair had tumbled from the pins that had anchored the heavy coil, and with shaking fingers she tried to pin it back, to no avail.

Etienne lay back on the couch and grinned up at her. "What a constant and delightful surprise you are, little one."

"What do you mean by that?" she asked, suspiciously.

As she stalled, not able to meet his eyes, it occurred to her that the way she had been acting was likely what she wanted, on some level, to do. She had thought it a dream, but she had a memory of him between her thighs rubbing against her and her own abandoned response, like a cat in heat. She covered her cheeks with her hands, devastated by the growing conviction that she was no better than her mother.

His expression sobered. "Nothing, my sweet. I meant nothing bad, truly."

She glanced wildly around the folly. "Look at this place," she cried. "It is so dirty! Filthy! How can you live like this?" She took the broom and cleaned up some scattered leaves that had blown in through the open window and piled his dirty dishes on the small table. She could not abide mess, and she whirled through the place cleaning, uncomfortably aware of Etienne's gaze on her as she worked.

Finally, though, the place tidied to her requirements, she slowed her pace and put away the broom. She met his eyes and bit her lip, hoping she would not see in his eyes the condemnation that she was just like her mother.

He patted the sofa beside him. She approached cautiously and sat gingerly down. He put his arm around her and pulled her close until their thighs were touching. "Little one—please do not take offense that I still call you that; I am fully aware that you are not a child but a woman—what you feel is not dirty."

She gazed at him trustingly, and his heart was deeply touched. She had become so much to him that he was no longer aware of what exactly it was he felt for her. No woman had touched his heart since his mother had died, and he wondered if his long string of plump, older lovers had all been an effort to replace in his heart the one woman who cared for him as no other. But never had he allowed them into his heart. Not even Emily, whom he had liked and respected.

But May . . . her laughter, her sorrow, her sweet tender passion were all life to him, and he thought that he would have to leave very soon, for the danger he brought her was more than just Delisle and his henchman. If they should fall in love with each other—what a joke, when he had thought he did not believe in love—but if it should happen, there could be no happy resolution, no fairy-tale ending. He was outside of the law, and he brought danger with him. And even beside that, he was poor and she rich. He could never marry with that between them. Marry? Bah, what was he even thinking! Marriage was not, nor ever had been, a part of his plans.

He returned his thoughts to what he wanted her to know.

"What goes on between a man and a woman is not dirty. How can you think that, if you believe in a good and benevolent God who created us as we are? You English do believe that, eh?"

"You have not heard some of the sermons I have, about hellfire and damnation," she said, wryly.

He was glad to see her sense of humor returning. But still, if there was one thing he could do for her it was this, and it might change the direction of her life if she believed him. "Little one, do you think that God, or nature, or whatever you believe in, meant love to be distressing to a woman, only pleasurable for a man? No. Lovemaking is meant to be enjoyed equally by both men and women. It is just that the consequences of that physical expression of love outside of marriage is so much more devastating to women.

"That is why there is this curious . . . *dichotomie* . . . ah, dichotomy—how strange that many of your English words are so like the French—there is this dichotomy between what women feel, and what they are allowed to do by society."

"What do you mean?"

Her open gaze made his heart turn over again, and he looked away. His voice, when he spoke, was curiously husky. "Men, dictatorial beasts that they are, feel the need for the virgin bride, you know this? We are a jealous breed. But for the woman's sake, for her pleasure, it is best if the man has had some experience before taking her . . . her virginity."

"Why is that?"

Dieu! Had nobody told this girl anything?

"You don't really want me to explain, do you?" he asked, shaking his head in wonder.

She pursed her mouth and looked off out the window, at leaves carried on the autumn breeze, and then gazed back up into his eyes. "I . . . I think I do, Etienne, if it isn't too much trouble."

Inwardly he groaned. Tell this girl about men and women, even while his body still desired her, while he remembered her kisses and her body arched against his own, her curves fit against his hardened body?

But he would do anything for her. Anything she asked.

"Let us lie back in comfort then, and I will tell you some of what is true between a man and a woman, as I know it."

Ten

Etienne watched May ride away on her pretty dun mare, Cassiopeia. My, but she had the perfect seat on a horse, and the view of her bottom . . . ah, he was becoming obsessed, and that was not healthy. He hoped he had answered some of her questions regarding men and women, but *Dieu* it was difficult! He must conceal from her the way he had come to feel. She must think that the desire he so obviously felt for her was merely the transient urges a man experienced when he thought about women or saw something that appealed to him.

She must never know the depth of his feeling. He could not quite understand it himself. Somehow he had gone from amused affection to . . . no, he would not say it. Perhaps it was just gratitude, for he had much to thank her for, and he would not be the first man to confuse his feelings. Relations between men and women were difficult, for always, in a man was the awareness of desire, the viewing of the woman with the question in his mind—and what would this one be like under the covers?

It might be the briefest of thoughts, but if there was attraction at all it inevitably occurred. He would not allow himself to believe it was more than that. He stared down the path, not able to see May any longer but unwilling to move. Who did he think he was fooling? He wanted her body, yes, but also he wanted her . . . he wanted her to love him just a little. And he must never reveal himself to her, never let her know his desire!

What *she* felt was the awakening of her young body to sensations she had long suppressed. Something had happened, he thought, that had shocked her, for her questions were quite pointed on occasion. She even wanted to know if people talked while they were doing what they did in bed. Or did they just cry out, unintelligibly?

How difficult to answer was that? For in his experience every woman was different. Some were vocal, chattering the whole time. That kind of woman drove him to distraction! Some said nothing at all, nor did they move or participate. Never did he make love to *that* woman twice. But some were the right blend, murmuring or sighing their pleasure into his ear, and taking delight sometimes quietly and sometimes with cries of joy. Would the little one be like that? He rather thought she would, from the way she had whispered his name, a sound so precious he thought he could listen forever.

And he must put that out of his mind. He would not be the one to give her her first experience as a woman. He was laying the foundation for a happy marriage for her in the future, preparing her for some other man's bed. With a bitter, metallic taste flooding his mouth, he pushed away from the door and threw himself back down on the couch.

* * *

May wound her way through the woods, and then let Cassie have her head as they cantered up the hill. Etienne had explained so much. It was odd that even though she knew her feelings for him were not appropriate, not . . . right, she felt comfortable enough with him to ask questions and speak of things she thought would be hidden in her mind forever. He made it all sound so simple, so delightful even, and it would take a while to assimilate all he had said.

He had explained the physical aspect of lovemaking, and it filled her with wonder. Of course she had understood some of the raw facts already. One could not live in the country and not know, unless one was a sheltered young miss, and she had been unusually free as a girl with a mother who was more interested in her endless stream of beaus than in her child. So she knew the earthy truth about animal impregnation.

And then there was Beaty of course, and what had gone on behind the door. . . .

But Etienne's description had made it seem not so foreign or strange. He had explained simply the facts of male and female mating. In his words it became natural and even beautiful, rather than ridiculous and sordid, as she had come to think of that when she allowed herself to think of it at all.

But she had not been able to ask some questions. For example she could not ask him if what she felt for him meant that she wanted him to . . . No, she would not even think it! She set Cassie to galloping, but then reined her back when they came in sight of the stables. She jumped from the mare and led her by the reins.

At night, lately, she had felt a confusing swarm of

desire and urges that had all begun to center on Etienne. In the dark she would picture his lithe form, his broad shoulders and slender hips and exciting hands, and she would feel the thrill of excitement, the heat as she remembered their kisses and how their bodies fit together as one.

But how could she want a man that way? Was it not disgusting, distasteful? Shouldn't it be if she was a lady? Not according to Etienne. But then everything he said went against the strict teachings of Miss Parsons. If she believed her friend, what she felt was normal, natural, nothing to be ashamed of. But if she believed her former teacher, what she desired made her a strumpet, just like her mother.

It was all too much to take in! Every idea of her life was being overturned, and she didn't quite know what to make of it. Etienne had not spoken of love, but then he had told her once that he did not believe in love. For some reason, that memory filled her with overwhelming sadness.

With a little shock she realized that she had not told Etienne that there was a distinct possibility, despite her orders, that her grounds would be searched. Her stomach clenched. If they should come upon him unprepared . . . oh, she would never forgive herself! But they wouldn't do it before tomorrow, and she would ride out first thing in the morning and warn him.

She led Cassie into the stable, and Zach ran out to take the reins.

"Give her an extra portion of mash tonight," May said, stroking the honey-colored nose of her sweet mare. "I've been working her hard lately, and she seems a bit peaked." Not to mention far too interested in a certain coal black stallion. She had come out of the folly to find the two together, as they often were. Théron had whickered gently, nuzzled Cassie, and then disappeared back into the forest.

May frowned as she noticed a couple of strange horses in the stable and an old carriage parked near the back. Maybe Dodo had company, though who would come all the way down to Kent unnanounced?

She strolled up to the house, but before she could go in the back way, her usual entry when she was in breeches, she heard her name called out. She glanced around. Standing in the garden, dressed modestly in a day gown of deep green, was her mother!

Her mother. Here, at Lark House.

She stood and stared at her, and Maisie van Hoffen walked toward her with a fearful look on her face. The older woman stopped about three feet from her daughter and gazed at her as if she could not get enough of the sight.

"Oh, May," she said at last. "How good you look! Even in breeches!" She laughed, but there were tears in her voice.

"M-mother . . . I . . ."

"I know I should not have come before you gave me permission."

"No. You should have waited," May said, baldly. She gazed at her mother, trying to hold on to the coldness she had come to feel toward her mother. But she could not help but notice the modesty of her gown, and the lack of paint on her face. And she was letting the natural color of her hair come in, the faded auburn that was like her daughter's rather than the bright henna of bygone days. It still did not look natural, but that likely would take time.

Hesitantly, Maisie took another step forward. "To be honest," she said, "I was afraid you would tell me I was not welcome. And I knew you would have every right."

May was silent. She tapped her crop against her boot and chewed her bottom lip.

"But I had to come," Maisie continued. "I had news that I had to tell you in person. May, I am getting married."

Eleven

Adorned in the gown that Etienne had approved—
it gave her a warm feeling to wear it now—May came
down to tea. Dodo had gone into the village to con-
sult, she said, with Isabel Naunce about the coming
festival. May had a feeling, though, that the vinegary
spinster had chosen that excuse rather than take tea
with May's mother, whom she could not abide.

Maisie was already in the drawing room, and the
tea tray had arrived. May stood at the door for a moment, observing her mother before she moved into
the room. The older woman's expression was pensive
as she gazed out the window toward the greenhouses
that supplied Lark House with out-of-season produce
and cut flowers. She was still wearing the dark green
gown. It was very flattering to her lush figure, but not
immodestly so. Maisie van Hoffen had been wont, in
previous times, to wear unsuitably low-cut day gowns,
gaudy jewels, no petticoats . . . anything to gain male
attention.

Was she playing a game, this time? Was she trying
to get her daughter to loosen the purse strings? For
that had been another condition after the disaster the
previous spring. May did not legally come into her
inheritance until she turned twenty-five or until she
married. But her mother had signed over her control

of her daughter's money to their family solicitor in return for no further action in the terrible case of her daughter's kidnapping.

So was she putting a modest face on, to try to convince her daughter that she was a reformed character? May walked slowly into the room and stood before her mother. Maisie turned, suddenly aware of her daughter's presence. There was a trickle of tears down one cheek, but she hastily wiped it away with one quick movement. She made no comment, nor did she draw attention to her display of emotion. Again, that was unlike Maisie van Hoffen, who had a dramatic way of expressing her emotions and used them to draw attention to herself on every possible occasion.

She stood and gazed at her daughter. "May, you look so lovely! I . . . I like that color on you. Gold suits your coloring beautifully, much better than gray."

May had always worn the most severe of dresses and the drabbest of coloring. It had helped her evade the amorous attentions of her mother's male admirers if she faded into the background, and she had come to think of herself as colorless, too, as well as her clothing. They both sat down, the silence between them awkward.

"I . . . I shouldn't have blurted out my news in such a bald way earlier. I apologize."

May nodded. It had been a shock, and unable to assimilate it, she had just said something about going up to her room and changing, and walked away without responding. What did her mother want from her, congratulations? Praise? Money?

As if reading her mind, Maisie said, "I'm not asking anything from you, May. I swear I just . . ." She made a helpless gesture with her hands, then dropped them on her lap. She busied herself with pouring tea into the delicate Sevres cups, and offered the dish of lemon wedges to May.

They sipped in silence.

"If it is what you want, Mother . . ." May started.

"It is what I need! A woman like me *needs* to be married," Maisie said, agitation in her voice. She took a deep shuddering breath. "I don't expect you to understand, May. You have always been so cool, so collected. Very much like your father," she said, with a wistful smile. "But some women should be married, and I am one of them."

May looked away. She was more like her mother than she would ever let that woman know. With her new understanding of relations between men and women she thought that her mother was probably right, that Maisie needed to be married for a number of reasons—not the least of which was the outlet for her physical passion it would have given her—and should have wed many years before, when May was still young. How much different would her life have been if her mother had married a suitable man, a strong man, giving her a stepfather?

"So why did you not marry long ago?"

Maisie put down her teacup and pushed it to the center of the small, low mahogany table in front of the settee she occupied. She glanced around the drawing room, calm and decorous in greens and grays with a huge painting of a hunt scene over the fireplace. Then her gaze returned to her daughter. "By your father's will, if I remarry I lose the very generous allowance I receive from the van Hoffen estate. I would have no money, no dowry, nothing, not even the jewels I wear, since they are a part of the estate."

For the first time, May realized that her mother was wearing no jewelry at all, save a pretty garnet ring on the third finger of her left hand.

"I was afraid to marry under those circumstances, afraid of what would happen if I could not stand it— being married again. I would never be able to leave, because I would have no money to live on." She made a helpless gesture with her hands, and then touched the garnet ring. Like a talisman, it seemed to reassure her, and she folded her hands together in her lap.

It was a day of firsts for May. For the first time she wondered what her mother's brief marriage to the elderly Gerhard van Hoffen had been like. She would have been a thoughtless and flighty chit, barely eighteen, when she married. Her marriage lasted almost three years before Lord van Hoffen succumbed to a putrid lung infection. What had those three years been like?

"But if you remarried you would still have had me, and the money that stayed with me as long as you cared for me," May said. "Would that not have been enough to live on? Even if your husband was . . . was unkind?"

Maisie's expression softened. She reached out and almost touched May's hand, but then drew back. "I would not live off your money, my dear. No, I make no excuses. I had a few chances, but I had sworn only fools married a second time. The money was only a part of it, the justification I used to myself to refuse offers. In truth, I did not want to remarry. I enjoyed my life, every debauched minute of it. Or at least . . ."

She shook her head and looked out the window with a sigh, before returning her gaze to her daughter. "I do not expect you to understand what I do not even understand myself. I told myself I was gloriously happy during those long years, and I had myself fooled, but I don't think it was real happiness."

May was silent for a moment, not quite knowing what to say. But curiosity got the better of her finally, and she said, "And now? What has changed?"

"I've met a man I can trust and love," she said, simply.

A ray of sun touched her face as it sank in the west, and May could see the fine net of lines around her eyes and mouth. There was lingering sadness in her mother's eyes, but there was also something different about her, a calmness she had never had before. But May would not be convinced so easily of her mother's transformation. Her hands clenched.

"That . . . that animal you took into your bed last spring . . . he . . . he said he spanked you and hurt you, and that you *liked* it! Is that what this man is like? Does he do those things to you?"

Maisie was hurt, and it showed on her face. In past times she would have let forth a stream of invectives, attacking like a cornered badger, but she swallowed once and said, chin up, "Mr. Banks is not like that!" Tears glistened in her eyes again, and she faced May directly. "I do not expect you to understand that . . . that time; I hardly understand myself! C-Captain Dempster led me down that road gradually. He was . . . was wonderfully inventive in the bedroom, and at first gentle. He told me I was the most beautiful woman he had ever seen, a goddess—that he *worshipped* me. I thought he meant it. I thrived on his words. I needed to believe him. When he first started the other, it was just pinching and r-rough . . . er, rough play." She flushed red.

But May was not going to let her avoid the issue. "And then?" she said, not even recognizing the hard note in her own voice. She had not realized how hurt she had been by her mother's betrayal until now.

"And then he went further and further. I thought I was in love with him. He interspersed the pain with . . . with gratification. And I think that somewhere deep inside I thought I deserved pain. I thought I was being punished for years of . . . of . . ." She covered her face with her hands and wept.

May sat and waited, waited for her mother to blame her, or disparage her, or something. Instead, Maisie dried her eyes with a lace handkerchief and composed herself, swallowing several times and staring fiercely at a gold and green urn holding tall rushes in the corner of the room. Her voice when she spoke was still thick with tears, but was controlled and even, trembling only slightly.

"I had been a despicable mother . . . less than that. *Worse* than that! And I knew it. Captain Dempster was my punishment. I didn't understand that then, but I have had a lot of time to think these last few months, and that is my conclusion. I was a horrible mother, and placed you in danger."

Her mother was taking responsibility for her actions? Unheard of, May thought. But still, a hard core of suspicion had not melted.

"And what about Mr. Banks? Is he even more . . . 'inventive' in bed than Captain Dempster was?"

Maisie gazed at her sadly. "I have done this to you, haven't I? I have made you suspicious of men and what they want. Not all men are like that, you know. No, I have not yet made love with Mr. Banks . . . Edmund. He . . . he knows something of my past, though I am afraid I have not told him everything, but he says that he wishes to start our marriage right. He is what I thought did not exist—a truly *good* man. I . . . I will confess my past misdeeds to him before we marry. I am determined to do this right, this marriage, and have what I have never had."

"But it still follows that you will be cut off from funds if you marry." What a fiendish thing for her father to do, May thought. She supposed he thought he was protecting his daughter in some strange way, but like so much in life, when one tried to manipulate the outcome of something, it so often turned to the opposite of what you intended. "Will you marry anyway?"

"Oh, yes. Edmund knows I will be penniless, and says that is all right. He can support us. He is an attorney, a friend of your solicitor, Mr. Standish. I met him when Mr. Standish was drawing up the papers last spring. Edmund has been married before—he is a widower of many years—and has a grown son in the navy, and he says the boy is doing well and does not need his father's support. He has a house in Richmond, a little ways from London; it is a lovely little house!"

"What do you want from me, Mother?"

"Nothing. I just wanted you to know."

"So you have made up your mind?"

She nodded. "I'm getting older, May. Edmund wants me, and he has such plans! He has put some money aside, and he is going to pay for the wedding himself. No elaborate ceremony, just something simple, at the home of friends of his."

There was silence for a minute. Maisie gazed steadily at her daughter, the expression in her eyes troubled. "May, *truly* I don't expect anything from you. I know I hurt you; I know I put you in unforgivable danger, and I will never forget that. There are no adequate words to say how sorry I am. If I could take it all back I would, but we are not given the opportunity to take back all the vile, vicious things we have done in our lives. All I can do is say that from the core of my heart, I am sorry. I never knew how much I loved you until I realized how horrible I had been to you. Someday, I hope you will be able to forgive me, but I do not expect you to now. It is too soon, and the wound was too deep."

May felt her heart thawing, felt forgiveness welling up from some charitable corner of her heart, when she had long thought that she would never be able to forgive her mother. Maisie seemed so different, but how did someone change the habits of a lifetime like that? She needed to know that one last thing.

She looked her in the eye and took a deep breath. "Forgive me, Mother, but I must know. You seem so changed from your former habits. I have never known you to be without a man in your bed. What have you been doing for . . . for sex these last six months if you have not slept with Mr. Banks?"

Maisie gasped, and May could see the shock in her eyes. The woman had drawn herself up and her eyes flashed with momentary anger at the insulting nature of that question, and all it implied. But she clenched the handkerchief in her hands, and then calmed.

"I think I am not the only one who has changed," she said wryly, looking at her daughter with what might have been respect. "You were ever forthright, but I never thought to hear you broach such a subject! Well, I will match your honesty, and I admit first that you have good reason for asking that question, and I have no right to resent it. Since your father died I have never been without a man for more than a week, and that includes during my mourning! But it has been easier than I would ever have thought possible. At first, I was in shock. Everything that had happened left me profoundly shaken. That I would put you at risk like that, and with knowledge . . ."

She broke off.

"And then?" May urged, unwilling to let her mother be overwhelmed by the past and her own misdeeds.

"Well, I didn't go out at all, just sat and thought a lot about what had happened. Mr. Banks came to tea one day, after I met him in Mr. Standish's office, but he was my only visitor. I refused many of my old acquaintances. And then one day I realized I had not . . . had not been with a man for a month, that I could not imagine going back to that way of life. It was like slimming! I was proud of myself, and did not want to 'cheat' on my good record. I blamed my sexual appetite for all the ill that befell me, but soon I began to recognize it was not that. The feelings I had, the desires, were not . . . were not bad, just misdirected.

"One of my former lovers tried to reanimate our affair, but I realized then that it was just because he was between women that he really cared about. I was just a receptacle in which to pour his lust. He would leave me, as they all did, when someone more to their taste would come along. That is why my affairs never lasted long; they all went on to some other woman who led them a merry chase before succumbing. I never said no to anyone, I was so desperate. I did things with men for whom I felt nothing, even some for whom I felt an active dislike. It was not passion, it was desperation.''

Her voice was bitter with self-recrimination.

"But then Mr. Banks began to call more often. We talked! Oh, we talked for hours. He loves gardening, and you know how I like flowers! His home in Richmond has the sweetest walled garden, and he has such a talent with orchids and roses! He is a genius. And he is so handsome. May, you would like him.''

Maisie's voice was filled with love and pride, and for one brief moment May was bitter that it took a man to make her mother change her ways, when it should have been the responsibility of caring for her daughter that made her more circumspect. But resolutely, she turned away from bitterness. That would serve only to hurt herself in the end.

"He sounds wonderful," she said, simply.

"He is! I so look forward to marriage; I who never thought I would say such a thing! I . . . I found that all of my desire for sexual release had become converted into desire for just one man. And though the marriage bed will be satisfying, it is not mostly what I want from Edmund. I want his love, and I wish to earn his respect.''

Was this her mother? May gazed at the woman before her and thought that all that time, when Maisie was trying so hard to retain her youth with paint and henna and youthful fashions, she had seemed so old, so weary, sometimes. But now with joy in her voice and tears in her eyes, she looked . . . well, not eighteen, certainly, but there was a sparkle of what she must have been like before life changed her.

"May, will you . . . would you consider coming to

the wedding? I would so like you to meet Edmund. I have told him much about you. How smart you are, how brave!" Her voice held an unmistakable note of motherly pride.

And then, unexpectedly, joy welled into May's heart, taking the place of the pain of her mother's betrayal. For this woman to give up her jewels, her London house, her allowance from the van Hoffen estate . . . she must be in love, and she must have made a determined effort to change. And if Lady Maisie van Hoffen, soon to be just Maisie Banks, could change, then May could forgive and forget. The past was dead and she would not let old fear and bitterness taint her life.

"I . . . I will try to come, Mother," she said slowly, thinking about Etienne, and his need of her. He had regained much of his strength, but the wound was not healing as it should, and she would never consider leaving him until he could fend for himself. "Can you . . . can you stay awhile?"

"Only overnight," Maisie said with a rueful laugh. "The wedding might be small, but it is surprising how much preparation there is, and I am doing it all myself. I didn't pack more than enough for one night anyway. I wasn't sure how you would receive me." She gazed at her daughter with fondness. "I would never have believed you would be so kind to me." Her eyes widened as she realized the implication behind her words. "Not that I did not think you kind, but you had so much reason to be resentful and I would not have blamed you if you tossed me out . . . not that I ever thought you would . . ."

"I understand what you are trying to say, Mother," May said, with a smile.

Maisie sighed with relief. Then her face lit with a mischievous smile. "I am trying to . . . trying to . . . oh, you will laugh at me! I am trying to learn how to cook, at this late stage in my life!"

May gazed at her mother in astonishment, at the woman who was emerging from the chrysalis of who she was. It was like she was being reborn. The woman before her had learned that sacrifice often had rewards, and that self-restraint led to self-respect. She longed to hug this new woman, but was still shy, still unsure. Maybe that would come with time. She needed to learn to trust her, and her mother would have to earn that trust. But she had a feeling she would. She *hoped* she would.

One thing she determined: Maisie would not go to her new husband empty-handed. On the day of her marriage, May would make sure that her mother received a letter of intent from their solicitor, telling her that in one year, on May's twenty-fifth birthday, ten thousand pounds would be placed at Maisie's disposal as a dowry.

"I am so happy for you, Mother," she said, and never had she meant anything so fervently.

Twelve

Dinner was almost festive. Dodo, reserved at first in Maisie's presence, soon relaxed, once she took in the changes in the woman's demeanor. The elderly woman had the mother and daughter almost in tears from laughter, as she described an encounter in the village with a local.

"And then when I asked him the donkey's name, he scratched his head, looked puzzled, and said, 'Don't rightly know, milady, as we hain't never been properly introduced!' "

Even Maisie laughed, and the dining room was filled with the merry sound of conviviality. May glanced from woman to woman. Never would she have thought to see a day when the dining room of Lark House would be inhabited only by women, and them having a delightful time. She remembered all of the years when she despised dinnertime, for her mother never had less than three men staying, and inevitably one would think it his duty to pay court to the plain daughter. After all, she was rich, and would make a convenient wife.

But tonight was a time to put aside painful memories, and hope that the future would prove different. The only thing she would change about this night was that she would have loved to see Etienne at the head of the long walnut dining table. He had just the right demeanor, a blend of cultured, sophisticated manner and a bon vivant's conviviality that would set everyone at ease. The memory that he was alone in the dark, cold folly, eating whatever was left of his meager provisions, took all of the shine out of the evening, but she forced a smile and stood.

"What say we adjourn to the blue salon, ladies?"

They drank coffee and chatted desultorily, but May had started worrying about Etienne, and could not settle down. She fretted and paced, worrying. Did he have enough to eat? Was he warm; was he safe in the folly? If only she could think of a way to bring him up to Lark House, but even in the attic he could be discovered, and at least down at the folly he could look after his horse.

She paced the length of the blue salon, or saloon as it would have been known in past years. It was her favorite of the formal rooms at Lark House. The walls were blue silk panels set into white wood, each panel hung with a different scenic view of the Lark House grounds, painted during her father's lifetime. There was one that drew her attention, and she stood mesmerized before it as if she had never seen it before.

It was the folly, and had been painted before the woods had grown up so much around it. You could see the pretty stone structure amidst saplings, and it looked like a perfect setting for a Greek scene with nymphs and demigods cavorting, but all May could see was one tall, powerful Frenchman leaning negligently against the doorway, waiting for her to return. She turned away with a stifled exclamation. She was becoming entirely too caught up in Etienne. She must not forget that he would leave and she would be left alone. Alone. What a desolate word!

Maisie's eyes were on her, and May forced a smile to her lips.

"Come sit here," her mother said, patting a spot on the silver brocade sofa beside her.

May took a seat. Dodo was glancing through a folio of drawings, searching for another scene to needle-point.

Taking her hand, Maisie gazed into May's eyes. "My dear, I know I have not been much of a mother to you," she said with a sad smile.

May waved off her regret. "That is the past, Mother. I have realized that it is unprofitable and painful to live in the past. The present is all we can be sure of."

A tear glistened once more, in the pale blue eyes so like her own. "Thank you for that, my dear. But I will never leave off regretting what could have been between us. Despite what you may think, I was thrilled when you were born and I found out you were a girl. I had such plans! I knew you would have all the advantages I did not, growing up."

Would her mother finally speak of the family she had left behind? May wondered. All she had ever known was that Maisie came from a farming family near Manchester. She had come to London at a very early age, and because of her looks had become an immediate success on the stage. But she had never acknowledged her parents, and May had always thought there was some bitterness there, that she would sever all ties so completely.

"But more than that," Maisie continued. "I wanted a little girl to pamper and spoil. But your father saw to it that I spent little time with you. He engaged a wet nurse immediately. Said the aristocracy did not do anything so plebeian as nurse their own children. And he engaged a nursemaid, and left orders that I was not to spend above an hour every day with you in the nursery. Said it was common. Said *I* was common."

Here it came, May thought, stiffening. She will blame everything, every failure of her own, on her husband.

"And I *was* common. Common as dirt, in so many ways, like the family I came from. He taught me just how different I was, and I learned to distrust my instincts. But I should have stood firm. I should have insisted on caring for you the way I wanted to. But he was . . ." She shook her head. "Enough of that. I will not abuse the man, for he plucked me from obscurity and gave me a life I could not have even dreamed of. Without him I would have become a courtesan, I have no doubt. He gave me respectability, which I turned around and threw away the moment he was dead."

"You were so young," May murmured, finding with surprise that she wanted to defend that young girl from long ago.

"I still knew right from wrong," Maisie said, not letting herself off the hook. "When Gerhard died, I had the chance to live as I wanted. I could have started then to take care of you as I had wanted to from the start. But by then I did not know what to do. You were sick for a time after your father's death, and you would cry whenever I picked you up, and then the nurse would shoo me out of the nursery, saying I was upsetting you. And I believed her. She was terrifyingly efficient. I know now that if I had been persistent, you would have come to know me better. It was just the illness and the unfamiliarity that made you cry. But I did not know."

"But I could not have been ill for that long!"

Maisie shrugged. "I was weak and silly, a twenty-one-year-old ninny. A man came to visit in the week after your father's death, a man he had been used to gamble with in London. He was my first . . . my first seducer. I had never known that lovemaking could be like that—so active and . . . and lusty—and I was utterly entranced. And then he introduced me to a friend of his, and . . . well, there is only one way to say it." Her face took on a grim expression. "He passed me along to him. I thought I was being gay and sophisticated. Thought it was what was expected of a young widow. That is what they told me, and I had every reason to believe them.

"In the theater company I worked for when I met Gerhard, we had heard that the aristocracy was very loose, and once a woman provided an heir for her husband, or once she was widowed, a woman could take as many lovers as she wanted, without censure. By the time I realized that discretion was still necessary, it was too late. I was a byword among the *ton*. And so I pretended I didn't care, and descended further down a path I had not even known my feet were set upon."

May supposed that she could understand that happening to a naïve and foolish girl of one-and-twenty. But why was her mother telling her all of this? It was all so much chaff, blown away on long-ago winds and forgotten.

Taking her daughter's hand again, Maisie said, "I just want you to know that I did not intend your life to turn out as it has."

Sighing, May said, "My life is just fine! I am past all the troubles of the bad old days."

"Are you?" Maisie asked, searching her daughter's face. "Are you past it all? I want you to find a good life, and I cannot help but think that I have spoiled for you one of life's best experiences, the love of a good man."

Withdrawing her hand with a sharp exclamation, May said sharply, "My life does not have to include a husband to be complete."

"There, see, I knew I had damaged you! You will never trust men, and it is all my fault."

Irritated, May stood. "There is precious little in most of them to trust, it seems to me."

"But a woman should be married. And there are many men who would make you a good husband!"

And not a one she would accept, even if they asked, May thought. Or perhaps . . . perhaps there was one man she would accept. She would marry Etienne, if he wanted her and loved her. But there was no chance of that. He could never love her, and she refused to speculate why that knowledge hurt so very deeply.

"Perhaps," she said, gazing directly into her mother's blue eyes, "I have been changed by my life experiences, but you have forfeited any right to comment and you cannot regain that right, no matter how much you have changed. I appreciate your concern, but do not worry about me. From now on I am responsible for myself. Good night, Mother. I will see you in the morning before you leave." Turning, May said, "Goodnight, Dodo. I apologize for deserting my guest, but I am tired. It has been a long day." She swept from the room.

She might have known her mother would sooner

or later return to her favorite subject, that of her daughter's obstinate failure to marry. It seemed that finding a new husband had only made her more concerned that May wed, too. She supposed she had been rather hard on the woman, but really! Her mother must accept that May would do what she wanted with her life. She ascended to her room, to spend a sleepless night, worrying about Etienne and turning over her mother's infuriating words.

In the salon, Maisie glanced over at Dodo with a puzzled look. "I . . . I suppose I was a little clumsy in the way I said that?"

Dodo looked up from the folio in her large, bony hands and snorted. "There is no way you could have approached that subject that wouldn't have gotten your head bit off."

"I just want her to be happy!" Maisie moaned, twisting her hands in her lap.

"Then don't expect her to be happy in any way you would understand," Dodo said sharply. "She is her own woman, and a daughter anyone could be proud of. Let her build her own happiness."

Maisie cast her an unexpectedly shrewd glance. "I know you don't have much use for me, Lady Dianne."

"That has nothing to do with anything," Dodo said abruptly. "You appear to be mending your fences now, and that's all well and good, but as I said, May is very much her own woman now. Took her a while to recover from that awful experience last spring, but she has now, and nicely, too."

"I'm glad. No matter what you think, I have worried."

"I don't doubt it," Dodo said gruffly. She stared at the woman on the sofa with narrowed eyes. Could she trust this woman? Was Maisie van Hoffen—the Queen of Tarts, as she had called her once—really a changed woman? She supposed she had to take a chance. "I have been worried lately, though," she said. "About your daughter."

"Why?" Maisie looked alarmed. "Why, Lady Dianne? Has May said anything? Told you anything? Is she truly well? I thought she looked a little . . . tired, distracted, sometimes. She just seems different. I suppose that is to be expected, but the way I saw her when I first arrived! She had been out riding in breeches!"

Dodo sighed and crossed the room, sitting on the sofa beside the younger woman. "Until recently she has been very circumspect. When she went riding, she . . . she wore her proper riding habit and rode with a groom, but then one day, a couple of weeks ago, everything changed."

Maisie gazed at her blankly, but then she nodded. "I'll wager she stole a groom's saddle and took off riding without a companion!" There was a hint of laughter in her voice.

Dodo looked shocked. "How did you know?"

"T'was what she always did before, when she was feeling particularly wild and free!" She sobered. "It was only when I had no . . . no guests, and she knew she could come and go as she pleased without being . . . being accosted by a man."

Dodo got a glimpse of May's former life, and her lips firmed to a thin line. No matter how much this woman had supposedly changed, it in no way made up for a past of cavorting with unsuitable men, and allowing them to pursue her marriageable daughter with who knew what intent! "Yes, she has donned breeches and taken to riding out alone for long hours at a stretch. And she has fixed up the folly—I assume it is the one in that painting—with furniture, saying she wanted a little privacy and someplace to . . . to dream, I think she said."

Maisie shrugged. "That seems all right. This is all hers, you know." She swept her hand around. "She owns it all, the house, the grounds, everything. Gerhard left me only a provisional allowance, and that will soon end."

Dodo shook her head. "I suppose I am worrying where I ought not, but there is a murderer on the loose somewhere in the neighborhood, or so someone says. But May would not allow her steward and the vicar to search Lark House property. Very sternly warned them off, in fact."

"She is very protective of her property. Always she has had this fierce attachment for her inheritance. I never understood it myself. I do not like the country; I never have. Richmond will be quite far enough from London for my tastes. Trust me, it is just that . . . well, that protectiveness and her independence that will not allow anyone to root around on her private property."

Dodo nodded slowly. "I suppose that is it. I have spoken of this—delicately, you may be sure, for it is none of my affair, after all—with Mr. and Mrs. Connors, and we have come to much that conclusion. If it were any other girl than May I would be afraid . . . well, afraid that she had contracted an unsuitable alliance that she wanted no one to know about. But May . . . well, the idea is clearly ridiculous. I guess the real reason also lies in the fact that the vicar and steward, Mr. Dougherty and Mr. Crandall, insisted on treating her as if she had no right to determine what went on. She was incensed that they dared organize the search without consulting her."

"That is your answer," Maisie agreed. "May has always been headstrong; I see it as a blessing, for that and her courage have allowed her to survive some very nasty experiences. Is there really any danger? Should I be concerned?"

Dodo folded her narrow, blue-veined hands together. "I don't know. On balance, it all sounds very . . . far-fetched. Wild. The normal bogeyman stories we all heard during the war . . . you know, murdering Frenchmen, et cetera? I tend to discount it."

Maisie sighed. "Good! I would not like to think May was cutting off her nose to spite her face. Denying them the right to search the property in a fit of pique when there really is a danger."

"No, I am not truly concerned about those wild tales of a murderer on the loose. If I did I would feel it my duty to urge May to more cautious behavior. But lately she has been different . . . agitated, restless. I just thought you should know."

"I . . . I appreciate it. But perhaps she is just discovering herself, her freedom from worry. She has had little of that in her life," Maisie said.

"Maybe that is it," Dodo said. "I hope that is all it is."

The next morning May determined she would forget about her brief spurt of anger against her mother. It was her own life, and she would marry or not as she chose. Likely not. She could not see marrying anyone after the knowledge she had come to in the night concerning Etienne, and her changing feelings for him.

She longed to go to him, but she had to stay until her mother left. She had no idea if she would be able to go to her mother's wedding, and so this might be the last time she saw her before the momentous occasion.

And Maisie must have been anxious to go back to her betrothed and her plans, for she was already dressed in an attractive carriage dress of tan and ochre. They breakfasted together, and then May accompanied her mother out to the portico to see her off. Mr. Banks's elderly but still sturdy carriage was there, waiting.

They stood in the dull light of a cloudy autumn morning, looking at each other. Dodo had said her good-byes in the breakfast parlor, and so only mother and daughter were present. Maisie gazed steadily into her daughter's eyes, and then reached out to enfold her in a hug, tentative at first, and then stronger when she felt no resistance from the slim woman in her arms.

May felt the unaccustomed softness of her mother's body pressed to her own in a tight embrace. She consciously relaxed, and felt surprisingly good about the hug. Her mother released her and held her at arm's length, looking her over with maternal eyes.

"My darling daughter," she said, her voice softer than normal. "I am sorry I never did that before. I have been a wretched mother, but I do love you."

She held up her hand when May would have spoken.

"I don't expect you to answer, nor do I expect you to say the same back. But someday, when you really feel it . . ." Her voice cracked and she sniffed back a tear. "I would have you live to make yourself happy, my dear, in or out of marriage. I hope you can come to my wedding. I have left an invitation on your desk in the library, as well as my direction after marriage, if you cannot come. Mr. Banks asked me to tell you that you will always be welcome to visit for however long you wish at . . . at our home."

"I will visit, I promise, and with pleasure," May said, and found she was speaking the truth.

"Are you truly all right, my dear," Maisie said. "Are you happy? Do you want for anything?" She shook a faded auburn tendril out of her eyes and gazed steadily at her daughter. The sky was a leaden gray, and a light breeze had sprung up. Maisie held on to her bonnet with one tan-gloved hand.

May smiled down at her mother and sighed. Then she drew her mother into another embrace. "I am happier than I have ever been in my life," she said. It was true, after all, despite her worries and concerns.

And with that, her mother prepared to leave, climbing into the carriage and letting the window down for a last word. She looked at May and almost seemed to want to say something, but in the end all she said was, "Be happy, my darling daughter, in whatever way you can be—truly happy, as I am now."

"I will," May said, and called to the driver to spring the horses. They trotted off and the carriage trundled down the crushed limestone drive, through the trees, and disappeared from sight.

She reentered the house, to find Dodo waiting for her with a searching gaze.

"What is it, Dodo?"

The woman held a letter in her hand. Her dark

eyes snapped with worry and the paper crinkled in her tense grasp. "Emily is not well, and Baxter thinks she would benefit by having me there. But, my dear, if you need me, or if you are still . . . still worried about anything, I will stay as long as you need me."

May strode forward and clutched the older, thin woman to her in an embrace. If she had learned one thing in the last twenty-four hours, it was that hugs didn't hurt. Dodo rocked back in surprise, not used to emotion from May, nor physical contact.

"Of course you must go to her!" May said, her eyes wide with concern. "Will she be . . . will she be all right?"

"Oh, yes. I have every faith. Emily is strong, but Baxter says she is restless and it is getting harder to keep her abed, and she *must* stay abed until the baby . . . or the babies, are born."

It was still unknown whether Emily would have one or two babies. May gazed at Dodo earnestly. "Go to her, Dodo. And take my . . . my love. And my prayers."

Dodo heaved a sigh of relief. "I will go the morning after next."

Thirteen

A steady rain set in, and there was no way for May to get out to take Etienne fresh food and wine. She paced and worried relentlessly, but the cold October rain sheeted down against the windows, soaking the landscape and obscuring like a fine gray mist the far glade in which the folly nestled.

She would gladly have braved the rainstorm for Etienne's sake, but it would just have looked too strange to Dodo and the servants if she had saddled Cassie and rode off with supplies in the torrential downpour. It was vital right now that no one suspect she harbored a fugitive in the folly. Over and over in her mind she tried to remember how much food she had left him with. And did he have enough blankets? Was he warm enough? Did the folly roof leak?

And she had not yet warned him about the Bow Street runners.

The next morning she blessed the faint glimmer of sunlight she saw on the horizon, as, clad in her breeches, she saddled Cassie and rode off with a burden of still more blankets to ward off the October chill, and a large hamper of food, wine, and candles. She took a different path into the woods, worried that if anyone was watching her they would know where she went every day.

The wood was fragrant after the day of rain, and she could smell the earthy fragrance of dead leaves as Cassie trampled them underfoot. Eventually she slid off Cassie's back and led the mare down the unfamiliar path. Sun glinted off dewdrops and birds flitted from tree to tree; it was a truly glorious morning. Finally she came up a small rise to the clearing, and the folly.

It looked as it always did, a welcome sight as she tied Cassie to a branch and approached the small building. Etienne was probably still asleep, so she crept up quietly. The view of him sleeping so peacefully, his youthful face calm in repose, was one that she still carried in her heart.

She crept to the door and peeked in, but then forgot caution, staring even as she knew she shouldn't.

He was naked. He stood with his back turned, bathing himself with a cloth, soap, and the bucket of water. His back was muscular, tapering from broad shoulders down to taut, rounded buttocks. Dark silky hair covered his bare legs, but the skin of his back and bottom was smooth and pale, like a marble statue.

Some sound she made, a faint gasp or the sound of her boots on the floor as she stepped in, made him whirl around. She felt a deep red blush rise from some heated place in her body all the way over her breasts and up her neck to her face at her first sight, or at least first full sight, of a naked man. She should look away. She was being immodest—worse than immodest!

The worst sort of trollop would still not stare at the sculpted muscle and hard planes of a man's body the way she was. Her eyes dropped from the thick column of his neck, over the soapy hair-covered chest, down the path that the arrow of dark hair pointed, down to his loins, dripping with soapy water, and there her gaze stopped while a dull throbbing in her body quickened to damp heat.

He was splendid, *magnificent,* a muscled champion in a world of hacks. And the finest of stud stallions, no doubt, she thought. And then her eyes traveled back up and she met his amused look and the flare of something deep in the tawny brown of his expressive eyes. His breath had begun to quicken.

"You came," he said, unnecessarily. But the way he said it sounded like he had been waiting forever.

She made a faint sound, but no words would come out. Finally her body would move again and she whirled and dashed outside, calling, "I . . . I will wait for you to dress."

He kept up a conversation while she unloaded Cassie, his voice occasionally muffled as he pulled a shirt on, or bent over to pull on boots, and then he came to help her. When his hands brushed hers, above the top of her riding gloves, she felt a tingling in her skin. She glanced up, startled, and he met her eyes and smiled.

Then he turned and carried the heavy basket into the folly while she followed with the blankets. He seemed much healthier, but he still limped, and she doubted if he could ride any distance or run far. Maybe he would not go just yet. She *prayed* that he would not go just yet.

May spread out a cloth on the table by the window. "I am sorry I did not come yesterday or the day before, but . . . I had company arrive unexpectedly, and then it rained. I hope you were warm and dry here, though I fear that is too much to hope for."

Etienne watched her bustle about setting the table and unloading the provisions, filling a plate for him. She bent over once to retrieve a jug of ale from the basket, and he felt his body stir at the outline of feminine beauty and the way her breeches clung to her lithe body like a second skin. The sunlight glinted through the window and the loose blouse she wore allowed the sun to pierce it, showing him an indescribably arousing image of her young, swelling breasts. She was more lovely than any image of Diana, the Huntress—more enchanting than any London debutante or Parisian courtesan.

Dieu, but he had missed her. He had missed her conversation and her care of him, but mostly, he had missed her mere presence. She had been gone from him only . . . well, not even two full days, but they had been empty days without her near, and it was not just his isolation, though that undoubtedly played its part. He rather thought he would have missed her even if he had been surrounded by lovely women. He watched her thoughtfully, not listening as she babbled on about her doings for the past two days.

Instead he remembered her eyes as he had turned, and she let her gaze travel his body, and how she paused when she saw his male parts. There had been no revulsion and no disgust, just curiosity, and something deeper that had made him swell with need. It was a good thing she had looked up finally, or she would have seen the effect on him of her innocent, wondering gaze. It was torture, remembering that heated look, and he shifted, trying to accommodate his skintight breeches to his arousal. Most uncomfortable, it was.

They sat at the table, she on the chair and he on

the heavy basket that had carried the provisions, and she drank her ale while he tackled the food. He was hungry. The food she had left him had run out yesterday at noon, though he had been able to find some late berries in the brush outside. He encouraged her to talk, just for the pleasure of hearing her voice. It had a soft, low quality, and filled him with warmth, though later he would have been hard-pressed to remember what exactly she had spoken of.

She seemed more comfortable, finally, by the time he had finished his meal. He could not help himself. He was filled with curiosity, and so he gazed at her and asked, "And so what, little one, did you think of your first view of a naked man?"

Her complexion turned crimson again. "That wasn't my first . . . I mean I've seen . . . not all, but much . . ." She stammered and broke off, staring at him with wide alarmed eyes.

Etienne felt a painful jolt of anger and jealousy pierce him. Who had she seen naked? What were they doing? His eyes narrowed and he glared at her. "And who would you have seen naked?"

She shrugged and looked away, out the window at the last golden leaves in the glade.

"Who was it?" he said, sharply. He struggled to control his feelings, as he saw her questioning gaze. Then an awful thought occurred to him. "Did one of your mother's horrible friends make advances at you? If so, little one, you are not to blame, so do not think you are at fault." He took her hand across the table and rubbed with his thumb the soft skin. "Too often women are held responsible for the deeds of licentious men."

"No, oh no! It was not that at all."

"Good. Good. I am glad. And now you need tell me no more, for it is not my business." Etienne gulped the last drop of his ale and patted his stomach. "Thank you once again, little one, for your generosity. I will repay you your kindness someday, I hope." He watched her eyes, still wondering about the spurt of anger and jealousy he had felt at the thought that she had seen another man. It was unworthy of him, he knew, but he wanted somehow to be the only man she had ever had reason to look at in that state. How ridiculous he was being!

His feelings for her had become complex, and when he had to leave, to never see her again, likely, it would be a wrench. She had become vital to him, and it was beyond mere gratitude, though there was so much to be grateful to her for. Would he ever be able to repay the debt he owed her? For it covered the extent of his very life. He rose and took her hand. "Come, I would like to show you what I found the other day, before the rain came. I hope that it is not too wet."

He grabbed one of the blankets, tucked her hand in the crook of his arm, and escorted her outside. She glanced up at him sideways, noting the clean lines of his jaw and the spicy outdoor smell that emanated from him, as well as the fragrance of soap from his bath. Now she knew what he looked like all over, and it should have frightened her. Surely any normal female would have been scared witless by the sight of a naked man. Instead all she felt was a devious, winding thread of desire that spiraled through her, and a sharp curiosity to know how his body worked. It had not escaped her attention that between the time she turned away and the time he had called to her that he was dressed, his body had changed slightly. What had been flaccid, she now suspected was swollen, and she felt a secret delight that perhaps it was due to her presence.

It should shock her. It should frighten her, especially considering her experience with the awful Dempster. Instead it intrigued her. Was that normal? She would never know.

He was guiding her through the brush, around a hillside she thought she remembered from her youth, holding branches away for her and helping her under low bushes, even though he was the one with the limp. But she would let him be chivalrous, for it was his natural way, as instinctive to him as his innate gentleness. Her deep conviction of his nature was what lay behind her stubborn refusal to believe he had anything to do with the attempts on Lord Sedgely's life, even though it seemed to be unquestionable. Someday he would explain all to her. Until then she would just enjoy his company and try to forget about the day when he would leave. She could hear the stream, but he was leading her away from where she collected water for him.

"Here," he finally said.

The hill had formed a cliff and it overhung the hillside, providing a protected spot from which one could see the stream, and how the light breeze sent golden leaves tumbling through the air to be caught by the water and carried away. She hugged his arm to her side. "How lovely," she exclaimed, and he looked as pleased as if it was something he had built.

"I have been tired of the folly, no matter that it is pretty and picturesque. Come sit with me here," he said, spreading the blanket under the overhang. He sat and pulled her down to him.

She found herself nestled in the crook of his arm as they lay side by side, his length stretched out and touching her, their boots touching. It was as natural a position to both of them as if they were lovers, and neither of them seemed inclined to keep distance between them. She trusted him implicitly, and enjoyed the warm points of contact between them.

"Now," he said, firmly, "you shall tell me how it is that I am not the first man you have seen in his nakedness. I find myself with a curiosity about this that will not be appeased. Truly it is none of my business, but"—he shrugged—"I would like to know."

"But . . ."

"No, little one," he said kindly, gazing down at her with a smile curving up his lips. He cupped her cheek and rubbed his thumb along her jawline. "I will not judge you, nor call you naughty if you have been spying on some fellow. Curiosity about men is natural."

She looked up into his eyes and felt his length warm against her, and she knew that she would tell him everything. He would be the only person she had ever told. Perhaps it would feel good to confess a disturbing chapter in her life. She took a deep breath. He smiled down at her and pulled her closer to his body.

She pulled slightly away. She would not be coherent if she was too close to his body, especially with the recent memory of him naked, she thought, breathless. "I had a governess from the time I was eight until I was fourteen," she started.

"Yes, this Beaty you have told me about before."

May nodded, and told him about how Beaty was like a sister to her, letting her play, walking with her, teaching her. Almost more like a mother than Maisie. "I liked to play pranks on her." May laughed. "She didn't mind as long as it wasn't toads or snakes in her bed."

"She was affectionate with you, yes?"

"Oh, yes. I loved her. I could always depend on her, you see. She was the one who taught me, when my menses started, what it meant, for I was horrified at first."

His hand skimmed lightly over her curves, and he said, "Ah, but that is when a girl blossoms into a young woman, as you did, evidently."

His hand had trembled and his voice was husky. She sent him a quick, questioning glance, but he was gazing down over the stream and did not meet her eyes. "Anyway," she continued, "one day, when I was about fourteen, and my mother had her usual houseful of male guests, I decided to play a trick on Beaty. I told her I was taking the pony cart in to town to visit my old nurse and to pick some things up at the shops. I went unescorted often. I made a pretense of leaving, but then I ran back up the servants' stairs and secreted myself in Beaty's wardrobe. I was going to jump out at her when she came in to get something, which I knew she would. She was always sewing or something like that, and would surely need her threads or needles.

"I had just hidden myself, when I heard her door creak open." May stopped for a moment. She could still remember the cloying smell of old lavender in the closet, and the lack of room as she scrunched down in the wardrobe. The fabric fibers had tickled her nose and she had wanted to sneeze and had to stifle it. She had left the door of the wardrobe open a crack for air and so that the latch would not make a noise when she opened it. She did not want to alert Beaty to the joke before it was sprung.

"And what happened?" Etienne urged, stroking her arm.

The autumn sun beamed down on them under the lip of the overhang, touching her with warmth. She could feel the muscles of Etienne's powerful arm flex under her shoulders as he settled her more comfortably against him once again. She did not move away this time.

"I . . . I heard noises, and I settled down real quiet, waiting until Beaty was well into the room before I sprung on her. I wanted to be sure it wasn't just a chambermaid, too, before I jumped out. But I heard two voices when whoever it was came in the room. They both came in and shut the door behind them. There was some giggling, and then just some muffled whispers and a moan."

May remembered the mixture of curiosity and fear with which she had edged open the wardrobe door and peeked out.

"I looked out. It was one of mother's guests, a young man whom I rather liked, for he was jolly, and kind to me. He was standing very still with his head thrown back and his eyes closed, and B-Beaty w-was . . ." May shuddered. Etienne pulled her closer, and she went on, determined to tell him everything. "His breeches w-were undone, and Beaty was on her knees in front of him. And she was . . . w-with her mouth she . . . oh, I can't say. It was too hideously embarrassing."

Etienne didn't say a word, but she could feel his eyes on her, and knew she was turning several shades of red and quivering just as she had that long-ago day in the stifling wardrobe. But she had committed herself to telling him, and maybe now it would not haunt her, the memory of all she had seen.

"I . . . I could not look away. It is a miracle they didn't see me, but they were preoccupied, I suppose. Anyway, then the man pushed her down on the bed and stripped her clothes off. And then he . . . he did things to her. I thought he was hurting her at one point, and was ready to leap from the closet and save her, but then I realized she was . . . she liked it. She was crying out because she enjoyed it. I waited until they were done, not knowing what to do. But then they fell asleep, and I escaped."

They had been entwined on the bed, naked, and May had stopped and stared for a moment, at the peaceful happiness on Beaty's face and the tangle of pale, naked limbs amongst the sheets.

"After that, I could not look at Beaty without remembering. I begged my mother to send me off to school, and Beaty was dismissed." She had been so bitterly disappointed in Beaty, she remembered, because the woman she had put on a pedestal was no better than her mother. Or had that feeling only come later, when Miss Parsons introduced the notion that only tarts enjoyed male attention? All she could remember *truly* feeling in the days following her stunning discovery was a suffocating embarrassment at what she had seen.

Etienne was silent, but May did not dare to look up at his face. What if he was disgusted by her part in it—by her watching such a thing and not leaping from the cupboard and denouncing the guilty duo?

"What were you thinking, feeling as you watched?" he asked, finally.

She twisted to look up at his face. It was calm and serious. "I was appalled! Horrified!" she said.

"Were you really? Were you not the slightest bit curious about what they did?"

May swallowed, and she remembered—really remembered for the first time—what she had felt, sitting in that stuffy closet and watching through the open crack the writhing forms of her governess and her lover on the bed. "I was scared, but . . . but yes, I was curious. Especially when I realized that she liked it. I was fascinated even as I was frightened. And . . ."

She stopped.

"And . . ." Etienne prompted, moving to his side and gazing down at her as he stroked her arm. "What else did you feel? You can tell me the truth, little one, everything."

In a daze, May mumbled, "I was excited. It made me feel hot and strange, like I had a fever coming on. I could not sleep for a long time without remembering what she was doing to him, kneeling in front of him. I wondered what it was like."

"And you thought you were a horrible little girl for liking what you saw, yes?"

She twisted and started to move away from him. "I *didn't* like it. I was appalled, frightened . . ."

"And then you went away to school?"

"Yes," she whispered. "And . . . and Miss Parsons, the headmistress—she was responsible for our moral education at Maxwell School—she explained to us over the years that no real lady actually likes all of those bestial male needs. Only low women like it. Real ladies are above the needs of the flesh."

Etienne gave a hoot of laughter and then he leaned down with a gleam in his eyes, and covered her lips with a soft kiss. It demanded nothing of her, it was just a sweet, soft, affectionate kiss. She lay quiescent in his arms and then laid her head against his chest. She felt in an odd way emotionally spent, as if divesting herself of that burden of guilt and fear and embarrassment had left her empty.

"And what did you think when you saw me this morning?" he asked, quietly.

How could she tell him the truth? How could she tell him that far from being shocked or revolted as she should have been, she was curious and fascinated. She longed to cross the floor and touch him, to find out what excited women like her mother and Beaty so. Was it only that so-tangible reminder of the differences in male and female, or did it have something to do with what happened once the two were in bed together?

Gently, he kissed her again, and she looked up into his eyes.

Her gaze was so trusting, he thought. So open. She lay with him as if there were no danger, but any man would be liable to take advantage of her vulnerability at a moment like this. And he could, he knew it. He was skilled and she was curious. He had no doubt that with a little kissing and whispered words of love he could be inside of her before too long.

But how could he repay her sweetness with such vile usage? No matter how he ached to find completion with her, and even now the sharp stab of desire pounded through him at the story she had told, and the knowledge that she wanted to know what there was between men and women, he could not do it. He clenched one fist and fought back the desire he felt for her lovely body, the firm breasts pressed against the soft fabric, showing hard peaks that begged for his experienced touch.

Instead, he settled her closer to him and stifled his instinctive urges. "I will tell you more, my sweet, as I did the other day when I told you of the physical aspects between men and women. But now I will also tell you about what I have learned about women and their needs, as well as about men and their needs. Your Beaty was just doing what came naturally. It was not evil. Perhaps it was not well considered, but she thought you were gone, and she was harming no one but herself by acquiescing to her urges. I have no doubt that she would never have done such a thing with you in the house.

"And if you are curious, you may . . ." He swallowed hard, and then continued. "You may look at me or even touch me, if you wish to satisfy your curiosity with a man who will not sate his lust on you."

Her heart throbbed wildly, but she trusted him utterly and completely. They talked through the afternoon, as the golden light shifted and shadows lengthened across the forest floor. It was enlightening to her, but she knew that it was difficult for him, though he never once said so. He demanded nothing of her, only honesty with herself and with him.

Later, they walked back through the woods, arms about each other like lovers. They spoke of other things, things she had always been curious about, concerning his personal life. He had family, he told her, back in France. His parents were both dead, but he had two younger sisters, one married and one a nun. He had no property, though by rights he should. All had been lost in the revolution, and he was lucky to still have his head. So many of his aristocratic compatriots did not.

In the course of the afternoon she had had the opportunity to see that his wound was still oozing an ugly, festering, liquid. Back at the folly she redressed it with extra care. It was taking too long to heal and she worried that she was doing something wrong.

As she doctored him, she told him about the Bow Street runners and the threatened search of the woods. "So be cautious, Etienne. They may search even though I have told them not to."

"There are no Bow Street runners after me, little one," he said, as she did up his breeches and stood, a little flushed.

"There aren't?"

"No. Those men . . . I know who they are."

She stared at him, forcing him to meet her eyes. "I think you should tell me what happened last spring in London," she said. "We spoke of honesty. I would have that from you, Etienne."

"Someday I will tell you little one, but right now it is getting late. You must go."

"Etienne," she said earnestly, stepping forward and putting her hands on his shoulders. "I know you did not try to kill Baxter Delafont! You could never do something so vile; you are too fine, too good . . ."

"Stop!" he said, through gritted teeth. "I am not what you think; I am bad and I deserve what they want to do to me. I *did* try to kill him, and almost succeeded. I will tell you all someday, but not now. Go! It is getting late." He turned away and would not look back into her eyes.

Fourteen

Autumn had really set in, May realized, as the slanting of the sun told her it was later than she had anticipated. She had spent most of the day with Etienne, and then to be brushed off after he told her he *had* tried to kill Baxter Delafont! Men and their secretive nature!

At least he had told her a little of his life and his family, things she had never known about him. His mother had struggled for many years to raise them alone, as his father had died early in the aftermath of the Terror. He was only sixteen when his mother died, and for several years had taken care of his sisters alone, until the youngest joined the Sisters in a convent outside of Rouen, and the middle child married at the age of seventeen. May's heart went out to the young man who had worked at anything and everything to keep his small family together. And every word confirmed that no matter what he said, there was some explanation of his behavior that would not reflect so very badly on him. He was *not* a murderer.

She kicked Cassie into a gallop as she emerged from the wooded glade and had a good run toward the house. A spot between her shoulder blades itched, and May had the queer feeling that she was being watched. If those men should see her day after day going into the glade toward the folly . . . That was ludicrous, though, for surely she would have seen someone, if there was anyone to see. She shrugged it off as she rode up to the front portico of Lark House, and let Zach lead Cassie away. She decided she would no longer sneak through the back just because she was wearing breeches. Lark House was her home, and she would do as she saw fit.

The hall was piled with trunks. Dodo really was leaving, she realized with a pang. She would miss the tart-tongued old woman, but no doubt they would meet again. They ate dinner together, and though Dodo darted a few questioning glances her way, she never asked where she had spent the day, nor why she had come back with dead leaves clinging to her hair and clothes. She was grateful for the older woman's reticence, and yet in a way sad that for all of the months they had spent together, they had never come closer than this.

Was that due to her own coolness, or Dodo's? In a way they were very much alike, not the kind of women to inspire strong feelings, and she could see her future in Lady Dianne's life, the life of a spinster. It came to her then that the only people she had ever been close to were the ones who were not willing to respect the walls she had built around her heart. Beaty and Etienne. They were the only ones who had breached those walls, leveling them into rubble. They forced her to respond to their own affectionate natures, and gave her unstintingly of their gentle care.

That evening she spent some time writing a hypothetical letter to Beaty, for she now felt guilty for the abrupt way she had treated her mentor and friend after the incident in her room. After all, as Etienne

said, she had only succumbed after being assured that
May would be gone all day. Never could she have
guessed that her young charge would be in a position
to see the couple's lovemaking. And who knew what
she felt for the man, or what he had promised? Maybe
she loved him. Maybe he had promised marriage. Or
perhaps Beaty's passion was so strong it took no prom-
ises of marriage to overcome whatever reservations
she might have had. Love could do that, May thought.

Beaty never knew what she had seen, and so May's
sudden coldness to her and avoidance of her had sad-
dened her. But she asked her student in vain what
was wrong. May left Lark House for the Maxwell
School with the briefest of good-byes for the friend
of so many years. Her last sight of Beaty's face had
been of tears coursing down the soft cheeks.

What had happened to her governess after she left
their employ? Did she find another position, or did
she drift into that dangerous area for a governess with
no family, the protected mistress of the man she had
seen in Beaty's room that day.

Of course she did not know Beaty's direction after
all those years, but she wrote a letter and thought she
would very much like to learn what had happened to
her friend. Maybe her mother would know. It was an
avenue to explore; the past did not hurt so much anymore. If only she had told Beaty what she had seen
and given the governess a chance to explain, but her
own painful shyness had kept her from confessing her
trick, and the discovery it had led to. A wall was more
comfortable, and she had erected a stone one between her and her governess.

Dodo, finishing up writing out the last of another
knitting pattern she was leaving for Isabel Naunce,

was still troubled about her young friend's behavior. Where had she been for six hours that day? She had that folly fitted up as a hideaway, but what did she do there? There was a nagging suspicion lingering in Dodo's mind that there was a man in the case somewhere, but that was surely ridiculous! She knew May better than that, and the girl was coolness personified. If she had been one of those flighty young chits, throwing herself at everything in breeches like her mother, then Dodo would have seriously worried, and would likely have investigated. But May? She had no use for men, and had oft repeated that very sentiment.

So if not a man, then what?

She rose the next morning with no clearer idea of what the girl could be up to, but her worry for her dear Emily was too powerful a force to allow her to linger at Lark House longer. If she had been able to, in good conscience, she would have left long ago to attend to her darling niece's confinement. As it was she was even willing to commit the solecism of Sunday travel just to cut a day from her absence.

After breakfast with May, she trundled away from Lark House with mixed emotions. She had come to care for the girl, she thought, as she waved a handkerchief out the window at her young friend. Despite May's coolness and reticence, she had a good heart and winning ways, when she chose to employ them. She could also be stubborn, imperious, and secretive, but everyone was entitled to a few quirks. Many had no doubt said the same of Lady Dianne Delafont over the years. They would meet again, no doubt. In her reticule she carried a long letter for Emily from May.

The autumn weather was perfect for traveling, cool

and crisp, but warm enough when the sun chose to beam. They rolled along for a couple of hours and then stopped at an inn to water the horses. Dodo got out to stretch her legs, which kinked up too quickly for comfort. The curse of old age, she thought, wryly.

She was glad Bill Connors was driving her. He was a cheerful steady sort, and Dodo appreciated May's willingness to part with her head groom and coachman for a few days just to take her guest to Surrey. It saved waiting for her nephew to send his coach; that could take a while as his attention was understandably distracted these days.

The inn was a bustling one, a Tudor courtyard surrounded by half-timbered buildings that probably housed damp rot, Dodo thought. She entered the inn, had a weak cup of tea served by a cheeky barmaid, and then strode out into the sunlight again, smoothing down her gold carriage dress with her gloved hands.

Bill Connors was nowhere in sight, but the groom who accompanied them stood talking to a shifty-looking creature, a man of about fifty, sturdily built and with a rough sort of good looks. Something about the man made Dodo shudder. She tried to identify the cause of her uneasiness, but could come no closer than a vague feeling that the man was entirely too eager to talk to the groom, following the young man about as he watered the horses and checked the traces.

She approached the carriage and was about to get in when she heard the groom repeat to the man the name of Lark House, and its approximate location near the Kent coast. The other man asked another question, but Dodo had no intention of allowing the groom to chatter like that.

"John Groom, where is Connors?" she called.

The young man whirled guiltily and tugged his forelock. "He'll be 'long right smart, milady. He's jest settlin' up wi' the innkeeper."

"Then what are you doing standing and gossiping? Surely you could be better occupied with the carriage?" Perhaps her voice was a bit sharper even than normal, but her uneasiness settled in the pit of her stomach and gnawed like a maw worm.

"Sorry, ma'am. Right away, milady." He shot a chagrined look at the hostler he was speaking with, and hurried to put down the step for Dodo.

She watched the man smirk, give her an evil-looking grin that displayed a row of dark, uneven teeth, and then slink away.

"What were you talking about with that man, John?" Dodo leveled a stern look at the young man before her, and he reddened.

"Weren't nothing ma'am. He jest was askin' 'oo the swell was that owned this 'ere carridge."

"And? Did you tell him that it was none of his business?"

The man shuffled, and his fair skin turned an even darker shade of red. "Well, 'e sed as how he thought 'e knew 'oo it belonged to, and said t'were some feller name of Jones, an' I sed as how it were the property of Lady Grishelda May van Hoffen o' Lark House in Kent. An' he sed as how that warn't the truth, an' I sed as how it were, but . . ."

"Enough!" Dodo said, holding up one hand. "So you told him everything about your mistress?" She frowned, and cast the stranger a narrow glance. He was now desultorily occupied with pitching some hay into the open stalls that lined the courtyard. Why would the man want that information? He made her uneasy for some reason, but she could not think why. She had never seen him before, but something about his looks rang a warning bell in her mind.

"Not everything, milady," the young man replied to her statement, shocked at her suggestion that he would be so lax as to give away everything about a mistress he held in awe because of her superior knowledge of horses. "Jest where she lived and such, and that she were home in Kent and that you was jest finished visitin' there, an' were on yer way to Surrey to the Marquess o' Sedgely's country place, Brockwith Manor."

Dodo closed her eyes and swayed back. She would warn Bill Connors about his groom's loose mouth, not to get the young man in trouble, but just because he must know that there was someone so interested in them. It was likely idle gossip—it *must* be just idle gossip—but still, the coachman must needs be told.

As they drove out of the carriage yard under the arches that spanned the entrance, she spied the stranger again—drat, but she had forgotten to ask John Groom if he had at least got the man's name— leaning idly against the thick timbered wall. He was chewing a piece of straw, and tipped his hat with a grin when he saw that she had spotted him. And then he winked.

Fifteen

May glanced around the landing and found that she was alone. Good. She was going out as she had not, in the bustle of Dodo leaving, been able to visit Etienne, and even though he had plenty of food to last him days and his dressing was newly changed, she still found that she longed to be near him. He had quickly become an obsession—or perhaps that was not the right word. She liked everything about him from his most obvious assets, a stunning physical attraction that was overwhelming to her senses, to the subtleties of their relationship. Like how he seemed to know what she was thinking sometimes and how she could say anything to him and he would not castigate her for speaking her mind. Even something as simple as how their appreciation of nature was almost eerily in tune.

The overhang they had spent the afternoon under had been, she now remembered, one of her favorite places when she was young. The fact that he had found it and felt it to be a special place was surely just a coincidence, but it was one more thing they shared.

And yet this time her visit had a purpose, as well. He was going to tell her what he meant when he said that he had, indeed, tried to kill Lord Sedgely. She could not believe it of him, and must think it some kind of mistake until she heard his story. She would have wagered her estate on the honor of Etienne's character. He could not be everything he was, and yet be a savage murderer. It was impossible. But still it had given her many hours of soul-searching and gnawing worry.

She quietly stepped down the stairs, hoping her boots did not give her away, but stopped when she heard a commotion in the front hall. Stainer's cultured voice was interrupted by a young, high-pitched tone. Something was wrong, she knew it in her bones. She galloped the rest of the way and arrived in the hall in time to see Stainer trying to push the stable boy, Zach, out the front door.

"Be gone, you scalawag. If you have something to report, do it at the servants' door, as is proper. What can have possessed you to come to the front door like this?"

"But, sir, I tell ya, I hear'd a gunshot whilst I was in th' woods snarin' . . . uh, chasing rabbits. 'T'ain't nobody else t'tell but the mistress, for Mr. Connors be gone and John Groom, too! An' Mr. Crandall is nowhere t'be found!"

"Gunshots?" May said, waving Stainer away and bending down to the lad's height.

"Nowt but one, milady!" the boy said, looking up at her with frightened eyes. "In yonder woods, near where that little old building is and the gent is stayin' there!"

Her stomach clenched. He had seen Etienne! She should have known that someone would have seen him at some time. Had the boy shared that knowledge with anyone? She only hoped that Stainer either was not close enough to hear, or did not understand the lad. A gunshot! Near the folly! Her heart thudded with a sick thump in her breast.

"Saddle up Cassie for me, Zach. I'll investigate. It is likely nothing more than a poacher, but I must scare him off my land." May spoke calmly, but her whole body quivered with fear as she raced down the hall to the gun room, where she retrieved her hunting piece from when she was young, and loaded it. She had never been allowed to hunt, but had perfected her shot with target practice and was a fair markswoman. She had always kept her rifle in perfect condition, oiling it frequently, so it loaded easily, the pieces moving with efficient smoothness. God willing, she would not have to test her aim that night, but she must be prepared. They would not take Etienne.

It was twilight, and the woods were shadowy. She had absolutely refused Zach's pleading to go with her. She knew from his description where he was when he heard the shot, and she would not put a child in danger. It could be a poacher the boy heard, but most poachers used snares not shot, especially so close to the manor house.

Was it searchers? Was it whoever was looking for Etienne? She kicked Cassie to a gallop, but then slowed as she entered the woods, close to where she thought the interlopers would be. She heard them before she saw them. The brush was being trampled, and one man hissed to the others, "Be quiet, you fools! If he is here, he will surely hear you."

May walked Cassie quietly closer to where she thought the movement was, raised her gun to her shoulder, and shouted, "Come out of my woods this instant, or I will shoot until I hit someone!"

"*Dieu*, I told you you were as loud as elephants!"

"Come out, *now!*"

Keeping her eye trained on the trees, she saw first her steward, Mr. Crandall, followed by the reverend, Mr. Dougherty, and then the two strangers from the village break through the brush. Mr. Crandall looked sheepish, but the others looked by turns angry and solemn.

She kept the shotgun pointed at the strangers, for that was where the danger to Etienne had come from. They had almost been to the folly! They could have encountered him sleeping, and taken him without a murmur. Or did the gunshot that Zach heard mean that they had already got him? She swallowed down her fear. This was no time to let Etienne down. Besides, if they had got him, they would not still be looking.

Unless they had shot him, and he had staggered away and they were now looking for his body. . . . She refused to think of that. She summoned every ounce of courage in her body and steeled herself. Anger welled up in her at the presumption of these fools to search her land when she had made it clear that it went against her express wishes. She sat tall in her saddle, taking advantage of her towering height over the men, who were on foot.

"Mr. Crandall, what is the meaning of this? And, Mr. Dougherty. Surely if you were coming to visit you would have come by the road?" She spoke in her coolest, unruffled voice.

"You stupid bitch," one of the strangers murmured. "Y'got a dangerous criminal in these woods somewhere, and we mean to find him."

"Get off of my land," she growled, no longer constrained by politeness after that unforgivable slight.

She sighted along her barrel. "I will give you to the count of ten, and then I will shoot you for trespassing."

One of them moved forward but she gestured for him to stay put.

"My lady, per'aps you do not know the danger," the other man said. He was tall and lanky, with a shock of graying hair falling negligently over his brow. His voice was educated, but May thought she caught a hint of accent. "This man, he has killed, and like a mad dog, he must be taken before he does further harm."

"I said, get off my land," May said. "Ten, nine, eight . . ."

"But he is a danger to you and your household! He . . ."

"Five, four, three . . ."

"But . . ."

"One!" She shot over his head, the sound echoing through the woods, and he turned and raced through the woods away from the folly, to May's relief, followed briskly by the other man, who though much heavier, was still very quick.

She laid the shotgun across her lap and patted Cassie's neck, proud of her little mare for standing so still, even with the loud, echoing report of the gun. She glared at Crandall, who was turning to slink away. "You are fired, Crandall."

"But, milady," he said, turning back toward her, a whine in his voice. "That feller they're after is dangerous! A killer!"

"I do not believe in any killer on the loose. And even if there was someone in my woods, he could not be as bad as that vermin you saw fit to obey over me!"

"But, milady . . ."

"I told you I did not want my woods searched with a bunch of lunatics with guns, and I meant it! I will not be disobeyed because I am a woman! You are fired! Clear out your cottage by the end of next week."

She turned to Mr. Dougherty. Her chin went up. "How dare you do this, Mr. Dougherty? After my explicit instructions . . ."

"Surely you do not wish a wanted criminal to freely roam your woods?"

"Better the devil I know to the devil I don't know? I don't believe in the bogeyman, Mr. Dougherty."

"Lady May, please, my only concern is for your safety. I would protect you, if you would allow me that honor."

His expression was humble, his voice pleading, but May did not for one moment believe that her welfare was of the slightest concern to him. Too many times she had seen him looking around her drawing room, assessing the worth of the Waterford crystal and Sevres china, the Sheraton chairs and Grinling Gibbons frames. He coveted her property. He saw a spinster with few chances of marriage, and thought himself such a fine fellow as to deserve to wed her and gain access to all of her lovely money and property.

"Protection? I want no protection from you or any man!"

His eyes narrowed. "Could it be, my lady, that you do not feel the need for protection because . . . because you know who is in your woods?"

"And now you have offended me in every way you possibly can. Get out of my woods, sir, before I have my men fetch the constable and have you up on charges of trespassing! There is no killer on my property. Is it so strange that I do not want strangers wandering around my property with guns?"

His voice softer once more, he said, "You need a man to protect you, my lady! You are too trusting, too innocent . . ."

"I need a man for nothing!" she declared, shaking with anger. "Now get off my property before I turn my gun on you!" She lifted her rifle again and pointed it above Dougherty's head, her finger tightening on the trigger. She wasn't seriously considering shooting him, but he didn't know that.

Cassie sidled, sensing her mistress's anger. Crandall had already slunk off into the woods and was likely halfway to the public house by then, and with a last long look, the reverend turned and left, too.

May lowered her rifle and slumped in the saddle. Thank God they took her at her word! Her fury at their presumption had carried her through, but now the full impact of the confrontation had her shuddering with fear. She rode through the woods and made sure that both Etienne's enemies, as well as the reverend and her former steward, were gone. Then she approached the folly, heart pounding as it often seemed to do for one reason or another lately.

She threw herself from Cassie's back and stumbled into the folly. But Etienne was not there! In the failing autumnal light, she raced back outside and looked wildly around. Out of the forest, like a gorgeous panther in all black, came Etienne.

"Oh!" she cried. "I thought they had gotten you!" She ran to him, but was drawn to a halt in front of him by the look of fury on his face.

"How could you do that!" he raged, taking her

shoulders in his large hands and giving her a slight shake. "How could you be so foolish as to risk your precious life for me?"

Eyes wide, she gazed up into his twisted face, the tawny eyes blazing with anger. "I—I—I . . ." Stupidly, she could think of no words to say.

"You foolish child! Those men are demons, devils! They would have killed you if those two men from the village were not there to witness. How could you take such a chance?"

She pulled away from him, twisting her shoulders from his bruising grip. "You are just like all men! I thought you were different, but underneath you are all the same. You think I should stay at home, no doubt, and needlepoint!"

"Better the needlepoint than for you to . . ."

"I am not finished," she spat, her body quivering with rage, a reaction to the danger she had been in, and her fear for Etienne. "Men risk their lives every day, and no one thinks a thing of it. I am just as good as any man, and I deserve the right to be just as much a stupid fool as you!"

"I will not have a woman protecting me!" he said, haughtily. "I will not hide behind the skirts and tremble like a woman!"

"That's just fine, because I have no skirts for you to hide behind!"

"I can take care of myself!"

"You would have died of gangrene like a wounded animal if I had not found you and fed you and cared for you!"

She was right, he thought, his fury dying. He gazed steadily at her, at how her blue eyes flashed in the dim light of the dying day. And she was right that she could look after herself, the brave little one with the heart of a warrior. "You little fool," he cried, and grasped her in his arms and pulled her to him. He kissed her hard and then kissed her neck, muttering to himself in his native language, and then saying, "I was so afraid for you, little one. I did not know if those men would kill you, and if I would make it better or worse by revealing myself. Oh, my sweet May!"

Feeling herself melting into his arms as her anger fled in the face of his kisses, taken completely by surprise by his swift turnabout, she relaxed into his arms. She pulled his face up to hers and kissed him, their kisses deepening as passion flared. He molded her body to his, pulling at her bottom until she was cradled against his body. She could feel his slumbering manhood burgeon and swell against her, and because of his gentle tutelage of the day before she understood what it meant.

He wanted her. He desired her, as a man does a woman. Entranced, she stilled in his arms and thought about all that that meant, about how she should be frightened of his desire, but felt only joy.

Blushing, she gazed up into his eyes in the dying twilight, reaching up and gently touching his cheek. She had fallen in love with him, she thought, dazed by the new awareness. She was deeply and completely in love with a man who had no intention and no ability to marry her. Even if he wanted to, which he never would.

But he wanted her physically, she knew that now. He desperately wanted to love her body, and she now recognized the warmth in her own body as womanly desire. He groaned and buried his face into her neck and nipped at her skin, then worked his way up to her earlobe, which he nibbled and lapped at.

He wanted her. And she wanted at least once to experience physical love. In her spinster years to come, she would be able to remember how it felt to be truly loved. By him. Only by Etienne, for he was the man she would always love, no matter where he was and whom he was with in the future.

"Etienne," she whispered, as darkness closed in around them and the night sounds swelled into a chorus. She heard Cassie's soft whicker of welcome, and thought that Théron must have come out of the woods, for the mare only made that sound for the big stallion. "May I s-stay with you tonight?"

He held her face in both of his hands and searched her eyes in the fading light. "Do you truly know what you ask, little one? Do you know what we would do, what I want?"

She blushed even deeper. "After our very informative talks? I do. I know what I am asking, and I want you, Etienne, I truly do."

His dark eyes blazed with golden, tender passion. "You will not regret this, my sweet," he whispered, and swung her up into his arms. He carried her into the folly and laid her down on the sofa, lying beside her and gathering her into his arms. "You will never regret this, for I have so much to teach you that you have not yet learned. And so much to give you, of my love. It will not all be lessons, but a long night of given and taken passion."

He lowered his head, and possessed her lips in a deep, sweet kiss, and then let his hands sweep over her slender curves. "Ah, *ma chére petite,* but I have waited for this night."

Sixteen

Pulling away from her, breathing hard, he stumbled to his feet beside the couch. He stared down at her, his eyes glittering with some dark emotion she could not name. He looked tortured and she did not understand. He wanted her. Even now she could see his desire etched in the taut lines on his handsome face. Should she reach out and pull him to her? Should she be so bold, so reckless? She was tired of being prim and proper. For once she wanted to sample life, drink its draft deeply, savoring the wild flavor of passion.

Her mouth was dry and she trembled with the knowledge that after being with him she would know all about the secret life of men and women. No one ever spoke of it, but it was there, intangible, hovering between lovers, the very air around them charged by sexual awareness. The special glances exchanged when they thought no one was looking, the delicious awareness she felt in Etienne's presence—she understood some of it already, and now she would know everything.

"Etienne, please," she whispered, and reached her arms up to him. "Come and make love to me."

He groaned and clenched his fists at his side, beating at his thighs. "You have no idea what you ask, little one," he said, mastering his breathing with a Herculean effort. He looked up at the ceiling, took a deep breath, and then gazed back down at her. "Go away," he growled, and his whole body shook. "Go; run! I do not want you here!"

For a second she was stunned into inaction, not believing what she was hearing. "Etienne?"

"Go away!" He grasped her arm and pulled her from the couch, and then swatted her bottom. "Shoo, little girl. Go home!"

Tears of humiliation welled into her eyes, and she stumbled to the door of the folly. She cast one long look back, but his expression was implacable and sneering, and she raced from the folly. Cassie was just outside, being nuzzled by Théron, and she swung herself up on her mare's back and kicked her into a trot, later breaking into a gallop as they left the woods, the folly, and the scene of her humiliation behind.

Etienne slumped down on the couch and put his head in his hands. Haunted by May's sweet, wanton expression and soft voice saying his name, making it the most erotic word in the vocabulary, he could do nothing but wait for his desire to pass. But he did not think that would ever truly happen.

For the first time in his life he had wanted to be with a woman who had never known a man—wanted to be with *May*. But it could never be. She deserved marriage and nothing less, and he would not sully her innocence when he could never give her more than sexual pleasure. *That* he could give her even as he took his own, for she was a passionate woman, perhaps the most passionate he had ever met, though she had not been awakened to the full force of her sensuality. And oh, how he longed to be the one who showed her her true nature.

But he could never offer her marriage. He had nothing a young lady could possibly want or need, and she deserved the world. She was brave and good and pure and he was not fit to lick her boots. How very dramatic he was being! He wondered at this wave of indulgent self-pity. It was not like him. He had been brutal to her and hated himself for it, for the wounded look on her sweet face, but he had known in that moment that if he was not, she would stay, and if she stayed he would make love to her. Never before had he denied himself what he wanted, so he had little experience. It took all the effort he could summon just to send her away.

But he had no time to consider. He had put it off the last time it had occurred to him, but now there was no choice. He must go, as he should have long ago. Delisle and his hideous cohort would be back. Her very manner must have alerted them to the truth, that he was there, and nearby, and they would wait only as long as they thought they might be discovered. He had, at best, a few hours.

They were dangerous men and he brought peril to May by his presence. He cursed himself for his stupidity in not leaving before, but now he must go. He limped from the folly—his leg ached from the night's activity—and around to the back to fetch his saddle.

Had she slept at all? If she had, it had only been a fitful kind of doze, but now she sat on the edge of her bed, her heart thudding with a sick tattoo. Something was wrong. Every fiber of her being screamed it. But was it just her humiliation with Etienne still haunting her, or was there something more?

Those men! Etienne never told her who they really were. If they were not Bow Street runners as they claimed, then who were they? What did they want of him?

She was never going to sleep at this rate!

She slipped out of bed and into her Moroccan red leather slippers, and donned the cloak she kept in her room so she could take early morning walks without disturbing anyone. She slipped quietly from the room, trying hard not to disturb Hannah, her maid, who slept in the small room next to hers. Down the stairs and into the withdrawing room she crept, and then through the French doors that led out on to the terrace.

The cool night breeze greeted her, lifting her long, unbound hair. She hugged her arms around herself underneath her cloak and walked the length of the stone terrace. The moon had risen and hung in the sky, a great golden globe with that mysterious face that stared down on the folly of mankind. The landscape was gilded, glamour-touched by moonlight. Never had the grounds been so beautiful to her, and yet never had she been so sad gazing out at her land, so very lonely.

What had become of her life? She had everything she had ever thought she wanted. When she was young, before she went away to school, she thought often of all the things she would do to Lark House when she was older and took possession of her inheritance. She had always known it would be hers unconditionally on her twenty-fifth birthday, and had never intended to marry. All she wanted was to run her own stud farm and live in contentment, an independent woman.

Now she had her freedom, that precious, enviable quality that she had longed for. And instead of enjoying it, she had found there was something else she wanted even more. Or rather *someone* else. She wanted Etienne. She had fallen in love with a man who cruelly and brusquely pushed her away, just when she wanted him most! Why did he not want her? That question screamed through her brain. Perhaps she would understand him better if she had spent her years in London learning more about men instead of avoiding them, but as it was, he puzzled her completely.

It was an impossible dilemma!

She shrugged her shoulders under her cloak, unable to rid herself of that persistent feeling, that prickling between her shoulder blades she had first noticed the day before. She needed to walk, not think! She took the steps down off the terrace, her heavy cloak fluttering in the breeze, and walked the gravel drive around to the stables. She checked on Cassie, and then strolled through the gardens, withering now in the autumn chill.

But she could not keep her mind from returning to the puzzles that tantalized her. Why did Etienne reject her—and so rudely!—when he so clearly wanted her? With the new knowledge she had of his body and his needs, she could not have mistaken his arousal. He was bending all his will to *not* taking her! He had been with so many women; why not her?

He had told her once, on that long-ago ride into London after his heroic rescue of her from Captain Dempster, that he did not believe in love. He believed in romance and passion, but not love. She thought she had been careful not to reveal to him how much she loved him, letting him think she wanted only his body and not his soul.

Was that, perhaps, the problem? Was his rigid self-control a compliment to her? She paced briskly through the garden. Did he . . . no, she could not think it. But once it entered her brain, the notion would not go away. Did he love her? Did he love her so much he would not make love to her?

She pulled a rose hip off a low rosebush and pulled it apart, scattering the seeds over the cold ground. He had been aroused, and it had taken considerable effort to keep from doing what she knew he wanted to do—make love to her all night, as he had said. She shivered at the delicious, forbidden thought. All night, he had promised, in those few brief moments when it seemed she would get her deepest desire; they would spend all night giving and taking passion and love, teaching and learning together how to please each other. It frightened her and excited her more than anything.

But again she wondered, did he love her too much to make love to her?

Ridiculous. Absurd to think that if a man like Etienne ever fell in love, it would be with her! He was used to the most practiced and beautiful of lovers, and would certainly not fall for a country hoyden, for was that not what he had seen of her since she came back to Lark House? She spent her time in breeches, riding her horse, and probably smelled like the stable, when he liked to bed lovely courtesans who bore the scent of attar of rose. He liked experienced women, who knew what to expect of their lovers. . . .

Had she hit on something there? Was his reluctance to bed her just an aversion to maidens?

That was it! She paused in her perambulation of the moonlit garden, struck by that thought. It was a whispered fact among London girls that rakes did not dally with virgins. There was the danger of being forced into an unwanted marriage, and experienced women were likely better at whatever went on between the sheets. And Etienne was a rake who preferred older women as his conquests.

Perhaps she was quite mad, but she had a brilliant scheme. What if she told him she was not a virgin, that she had been with men before? Would he believe her? Would he make love to her? How would she explain all of the talks they had had about men and their needs? Maybe she could brush it off and say that she had made love, but had never understood all of the other things that Etienne told her.

It was the moonlight affecting her, surely! It was lunacy to lie to him simply so he would make love to her. But he would leave, and she would never see him again, and she wanted him so very badly! Desperation shivered through her like a cold chill. She rubbed her arms under her cloak and stared up at the moon. She would be a spinster all her life, but she did not have to die a maiden. She wanted to make love with Etienne and have that memory of him to warm her through the years.

Tears started in her eyes, but she impatiently brushed them away. She would do it, before fear made her cautious. She had nothing to lose but her virginity, and nothing to gain but a sweet memory to carry throughout her life. If he rejected her yet again, she would accept that he really did not want her. She strode back to the stables and quietly, silently, walked Cassie out of her stall, found a mounting block, and jumped up onto her mare's back, her night rail pushed up so her legs were bare under the wool cloak. She had ridden bareback before and Cassie willingly trotted down the moonlit grassy stretch toward the glade, her trot quickening to a canter as they neared it. She needed no guidance, and seemed to know that her mistress was going to the folly. Perhaps Cassie was as willing as May, for she was smitten, it seemed, with Etienne's big black stallion. Mistress and mount had fallen in love with gorgeous Frenchmen; may they both find fulfillment! May almost giggled with the absurd thought and the giddy feeling of anticipation that thrummed through her body. She rode toward the moonlight and the woods, her long hair fluttering out behind her and the cloak flapping, not noticing the shadow that slid after her from the dark area beside the stable.

The copse was dark, the light of the moon filtering only a little into the shadowy depths, and that only because the alders and beeches had lost most of their leaves. She should have thought of a lantern! Never had she been this impulsive, but now that she was set on this course she did not want to turn back for something as prosaic as a lantern. Not when she had Etienne to look forward to.

Cassie was restless and shied a couple of times, dancing sideways nervously. Probably there were small night animals out foraging. They picked their way along the path to the folly, avoiding overhanging branches. As the moon rose higher on its journey across the night sky, the light shone more directly down, and soon she could see a little better as the silvery light beamed softly through the branches.

There it was, the doorway and windows dark shadows in the mysterious night. She would be with him soon. She would lie with him and tell him he need not fear taking her, that she was no virgin—she was an experienced woman and she wanted him. If she could just convince him of that, she could have him in her arms. That was all she wanted at that moment. By the time he realized she had lied, it would be too late.

She slipped from Cassie's back and patted her rump. "Go find your handsome stallion, girl. Don't let him get away from you," she whispered. "And I will find Etienne. Tonight we will be together." The words echoed in the dark wood like a whispered promise.

She stole into the doorway of the folly and stood, waiting for her eyes to adjust to the darkness inside. There was something different about the folly . . . it was . . . it was tidy. Everything she had brought for Etienne was piled together with a note pinned to the top, and . . . the couch was empty! The blankets were neatly folded and piled at the end of it.

He was gone! He had deserted her, and she darted into the folly, crying out his name. But he was gone and there was no remedy for that, no calling him back from wherever he had gone. He would return to France and she would never see him again.

Pain seared through her breast, and she covered her eyes with her hands and wept, the hot tears pouring through her fingers.

She felt hands grasp her shoulders from behind, and for one glorious moment she thought, *He has come back to me!* but then a hated, well-remembered voice whispered in the darkness as fingers like iron twisted her arm behind her back, "Don't cry, girlie, just coz your Frenchie lover's deserted you. I'll give you what you're looking for, and I'll take your jewels, too. I've never forgotten that nasty turn you did me back in the spring, and I'll make you regret it, on your back, y'little tramp!"

Seventeen

Dempster!

In that one second all of the fear she thought she had defeated returned and all of the courage she thought she had gained fled. She remembered the loathsome sound of his voice in the conservatory that fateful night when he had drugged her and kidnapped her, and then, when she awoke from the drugs in a deserted, filthy hovel, he had told her in detail what he intended to do to her. He was breaking her in for the elderly Lord Saunders to whom, with her mother's permission, she was being given in marriage.

The old man had wanted a wife to provide him with an heir, but did not want to be bothered breaking in any squeamish virgin. It was a demonic plan designed to frighten her, break her spirit, and bring her cowed and subjugated to marriage. To her credit, Maisie van Hoffen did not know about that part of the bargain. To her thinking, marrying an elderly man was not such a bad end for a girl; after all, it was what she had done.

She had thought she was safe from Dempster, that he would not dare show his face again, but it appeared that she was wrong. He wanted revenge on her for her manner of escaping from him, which had involved pain to his private unmentionable parts.

May struggled against the hold he had on her, but he was very strong, as she well remembered. His fetid breath clouded around her as he muttered a stream of filthy words into her ear, calling her every name he could think of and telling her in incoherent detail how much he had looked forward to this night, to his revenge.

"Too good to be true, I thought it, when I heard you was in residence here, an' with no one else about. Thought you would of stayed in London. Chance of a lifetime to get a little of me own back."

"You'll never take me." She grunted, and paid for her defiance when he twisted her arm harder. She felt like the bone was going to snap.

She whimpered in pain, and he pulled her back against his body. "Now that's what I like to hear, a woman weepin'. Ya know me enough to know how that makes me nice an' hard. But then you remember, don't ya, how I feel? You remember, you little bitch, how you took me family jewels and dug yer nails in and like to pull it off?"

"I remember!" she cried, struggling in his powerful grasp. "I remember well! And I hope it still hurts, you bastard!"

"Bitch." He hissed, circling her body with an arm that felt like steel. "You're not worth bedding, you little tramp. I know what you were doin', coming out here in the middle of the night. Already been broke to the saddle, ain't ya? Gave it away to that Frenchie who came and got you that day, didn't you? Whore." He spat. "Just like your mother!"

Anger welled up in her and she thrust her elbow

back, catching him in the ribs. He expelled his breath in a whoosh and she tried to pull away from him, but it only angered him more and he twisted her arm higher, and grasped her around the waist so tightly that she was helpless. If she had had her riding boots on she would have stomped on his foot, but what good were Moroccan slippers to a booted foot?

"I don't want yer ugly body no more, you wizened-up spinster. Frenchie was prob'ly only doin' you out o' pity. I *will* take your jewels, though, coz I aim to have the money I should o' got . . . the money Saunders was gonna give me for breakin' you in and bringing you docile to him to marry. You owe me!"

May trembled, fear coursing through her blood in waves. But she was not that scared girl from last spring. Etienne thought her brave! She calmed herself and gazed around her, her eyes now accustomed to the dimness. Dempster was marching her forward, toward the door, but he was not going to control her anymore.

With her free hand clenched, she slammed her fist down on his arm, which clutched her around the waist. His hold loosened, and she twisted out of his grasp and looked wildly around for something to arm herself with, for he was now between her and the door, and the look of fury on his face told her he had no intention of letting her get away from him this time. The pale moonlight gleamed on something metallic, and she saw what she needed. There on the table, by the pile of clothing and blankets, was the straight razor she had loaned Etienne.

She grabbed it and held it up as Dempster advanced on her again. Had he really thought so little of her ability to defend herself that he had no weapon? But yes, he was unarmed, and she raised her hand with the razor while backing him to the door.

He eyed the razor, and she could tell by some slight movement the moment he was set to lunge at her to take the razor. She danced around him and raced from the folly, the cloak billowing out behind her.

And that was her downfall. He ran after her and grabbed a handful of the wool cloak, dragging her back. "You're not getting away from me this time," he yelled, his voice hoarse and harsh with anger.

She turned on him swiftly and he staggered backward, but still retained hold of her flowing cape. With one swift, smooth motion, May twisted the clasp of her cloak, undoing it, and as it fell away from her shoulders, freeing her movements. She darted at the staggering man with a downward slashing motion of the razor and connected with his wrist. He screamed and released her, and she kicked him in the stomach. He tumbled to the ground and she heard a thud, like a ripe melon hitting a rock, and then he lay still.

"Move, ya Frenchie bastard."

"Jem, shut your miserable mouth, before I shut it for you. There is no need for incivility toward my unfortunate compatriot."

Delisle's smooth voice and urbane manner grated on Etienne in a way Jem Foster's crudeness could not. "I will kill you, Delisle, if I ever get my hands on you."

A chuckle in the darkness was all the evidence there was of the older Frenchman. "My friend, if you had not seen fit to double-cross me in that little affair of Lord Sedgely, we would both be basking in wealth at this moment."

"I couldn't do it, Delisle! I am not a hardened criminal. Just very, very stupid." He had switched to French, and Jem squeezed him harder as he pushed him through the woods, and a tree limb slapped him in the face.

"English, you bastard. You're in England now, speak the lingo!"

Etienne felt a trickle of blood from the branch that had hit him. They staggered through the brush, and Etienne knew they were headed for the folly. He had almost made it away and would have been long gone, but he had stopped to write that note to May. He just could not leave without a word of gratitude and a good-bye. And it had been his undoing.

The quality of the darkness changed, and Etienne knew instinctively that they were nearing the clearing where the folly stood. Of course Delisle had taken away his pistol, but he thought longingly of the straight razor he had left on the table. If he could just get to it before his captors realized what was going on. . . .

They broke through the last line of brush and into the semilit clearing, where the moon shone down on a glorious and silvery sight Etienne was stunned to see.

It was May, her hair streaming behind her, and she looked like a Valkyrie standing over a slain foe. Her white night rail stained with blood, fluttered out behind her and she held the straight razor in her hand. And who? It was that foul bastard, Dempster, at her feet!

He took all of this in a second, and he felt Jem freeze in place as Delisle followed them into the clearing.

Jem might be a fool, but he knew what to do. He immediately pressed the knife in his hand to Etienne's throat. A trickle of blood spilled down his neck and under his shirt.

"Etienne!" cried May, and moved forward.

Damn, Etienne thought. His best chance of forcing Delisle to release May was if she showed no sign of recognizing him, but with that one agonized word, she had given away both her knowledge of him and the fact that he was important to her.

"I would not do that, my lady, if I were you," Delisle said, his voice a studied calm that was belied by jerky movements as he raised his hand and held it, palm out, toward her. He pulled Etienne's pistol out of his greatcoat pocket and pointed it at her. "One step closer and your . . . paramour will die like a slaughtered hog. And you will die by the bullet."

She gasped and in the moonlight Etienne could see how pale she was, and yet how very beautiful, standing over her attacker's body, weapon still in her hand. Her soft white night rail fluttered in the night breeze, and the wind picked up the tangled strands of her glorious auburn hair. So the evil Dempster had found her, and she had defeated him. She was worthy of a heroic ode, was his brave little one. Formidable!

But even as he watched he saw fear override her courage, and he knew in an instant that it was the sight of him captive, the sight of his blood, that had undone her. She had come to care for him. And what had he done? Brought her only danger; after she had so bravely fought her own battle, she must be entangled in his.

"She is not my paramour, Delisle," he muttered. The knife bit into his throat just a little deeper as Jem tightened his hold and he stiffened, trying to subdue the flash of pain. He saw the fear in her eyes as she watched the trickle of blood swell and soak his shirt-front.

"Is she not? Then you are losing your touch, my old friend." He eyed her appreciatively, his eyes traveling over her slender form. "Perhaps she is not to your liking, but surely she is worthy of a little tumble, yes? This moment she looks like a warrior maiden, and it would be entrancing to find out how such a woman would be in the bedchamber." His cultured voice hardened. "Throw that straight razor over here, my lady, softly, so Jem's hand does not slip."

She did as she was told, and Delisle bent his lanky body to pick it up. He looked it over and then glanced at the body of Dempster. "You are an enemy not to be taken for granted, I think. Never have I seen a woman dispatch a man in such a fashion, but"—he shrugged—"always there is a first time. I do not know the poor bastard at your feet, but I pity him. Is he dead, by the way?" He pitched the straight razor into the forest as he spoke.

May wondered that for the first time. She nudged Dempster with the toe of her Moroccan slipper, and he moaned and then lapsed back into unconsciousness. "H-he is not dead." She shivered in the chilly night air, and stared back up at Delisle, her eyes wide with fear.

"Not that it matters," Delisle said. "Now, I think that this is a fortunate occurrence for my friend and myself. I think you care for this rogue just a little, do you not?"

Say no, Etienne thought, staring into her eyes. *Con-*

sign me to the devil, little one! Do not give them a hold over you.

But May, her blue eyes wide and sparkling with unshed tears, nodded.

"He owes us, you see, a lot of money," Delisle said, watching the girl with calculating eyes. "A very large amount. We know that there is no hope of collecting it from him, worthless as he is, but perhaps we have underestimated his value. Perhaps we can simplify what has become a convoluted plot to regain my investment."

Delisle moved further into the clearing and circled May and her victim. "We have been in this district for a few weeks—long enough to learn of the thrifty and very wealthy Lady Grishelda May van Hoffen. Tell me, my dear," he said, moving close to her from behind and touching her bare hand and the streak of blood that fouled it, "are you wealthy? You see I only ask, though I know it is not done in polite circles, because if you are, I will give you the chance to redeem your lover's life."

Etienne stiffened and felt the knife bite into his flesh again. That was Delisle! Always he had an eye on the money, and always would he find a way to make a hopeless situation pay off for him. If only she would say she was poor! But he could see in her beautiful blue eyes that she was going to tell him the truth.

"I . . . I am very wealthy," she whispered, shuddering as Delisle caressed her bare neck and lifted her heavy hair off her back with the barrel of Etienne's pistol.

He buried his face in her hair, and murmured, "Mmmm, like silk. And fragrant, with your very English scent of lavender." He circled to stand in front of her, and his gaze raked over her form, taking in the rounded swell of her bosom and the promise of long, slim legs under the filmy night rail. "Per'aps there is more than just your wealth to entice my excitable friend here. You are not his type, and you are not pretty. He says you are not his paramour, but I find I do not believe him.

"Did he seduce you from innocence? How unlike him. I have known him some time, and never have I known him to dally with a maiden. Nor for him the untried virgins, you see." He spoke as if it were the common thing to hold a conversation like that in the forest. Then his gaze sharpened, his beaky nose casting an eerie shadow over his face in the bright moonlight. "You are wealthy. Is some of that wealth in portable form, jewels, gold, that sort of thing?"

She nodded, mesmerized by Delisle's cultured voice, like a rabbit listening to the soothing hiss of a snake. "I . . . I have many jewels, worth thousands of pounds. A-and gold."

"Good, good," the tall man said.

Etienne could almost see the greedy wheels of Delisle's mind turning, scheming.

"That's the ticket, ain't it then?" Jem said, his voice hoarse with excitement. "We'll get some good out o' this lot yet."

"*Bien,* let us go, then. You, my lady, will lead the way out of this wretched forest to your home. And no tricks or your French lover will be dead before your scream for help is finished."

Good, they were going to Lark House, Etienne thought. If only they would get close enough, and he would send her to the house and then shout the forest down, for he cared not what happened to himself, he only wanted her to be safe. It humbled him to know that she would give her worldly possessions for his worthless hide, but he could not let her do it. Nor did he think they would really leave him alive once they had the jewels and gold in their possession. The long, tangled skein between them was unraveling now, and Delisle would take the jewels, then kill him, and perhaps May as well. He must not let her be harmed.

May led the way through the woods. She glanced around her once, as though looking for something, and Etienne wondered if she had brought Cassie with her. Théron had bolted when Delisle and Jem had entrapped him and pulled him from his horse. There had been no time for the stallion to react, and Etienne was just glad his steed had gotten away. With any luck the mare had found him, for he was ambushed just on the other side of the woods, and his horse would reenter the forest for safety. Together he and the mare would be safe.

Finally they made it to the outer edge of the forest, on the manor house side. There was a long, broad sweep of land up to the back of the house and a long terrace. It was a ways away, but moonlight touched the windows, making them glint silver in the distance. Delisle took May's arm and glared deep into her eyes. "Now, my pet, you will go and get for us the jewels and gold, as much as you can carry. If you do not come back, we will kill him. If you alert anyone, we will kill him. And it will not be a quick death, but slow and lingering, and we will tear his hide from him first, strip by strip so that the grounds of your so-pretty home will ring with the screams!"

She shuddered and whimpered, and Etienne cursed the man's viciousness.

"Enough, Delisle! Do not frighten her or I will . . ."

"You will what?" The man snarled, turning his basilisk gaze on Etienne.

Impotent fury coursed through Etienne. In the struggle with the bastards, his groin had been reinjured and ached fiercely. He was weak, still, and no contest for two men. And they had stopped far enough away that no yelling on his part could be certain of being heard. He tried to catch May's eye, and she looked his way.

He shook his head, and nodded toward Delisle. *Dieu,* if only he could say what he wanted! *Do not do what they say! Stay safely in the house and arm your male staff. Worry not about me. Do not come back for me!* He wanted to scream it, and tried to pour the message into his eyes.

And even if she did come back it would be useless, for they would kill him anyway, and likely her, too. But he dared not say aloud what he thought, for they would not let her go if they thought she would not come back.

He had a brainstorm. It was flimsy and wretched, but it was his only hope of giving her the message without endangering her. "Little one," he said, carefully, staring into her beautiful blue eyes. "Listen to me. Be sure and bring back for them the one special necklace. The one of sapphire, tourmaline, agate, and . . . and yellow gold. You remember, the one you told me of? Sapphire, tourmaline, agate, and yellow . . . gold. And then you will be *safe.*"

S-T-A-Y. Stay, he thought, fiercely. *Once you are safe, stay!*

She frowned at him. She seemed aware that he was

trying to tell her something, but not sure what it was. Delisle's eyes narrowed in suspicion.

"Move, my lady!" he said, his voice hoarse and commanding.

Etienne gazed into her eyes, and then he saw dawning understanding. She moved toward him while Jem tightened his hold and muttered that she had better not do anything foolish.

Tenderly, she looked into his eyes and her blood-stained hand came up to caress his cheek. Her hand was trembling and cold, and he turned his lips in to her palm and kissed it fervently, hoping as he did that she would never know what he felt for her. As much as he cared, he must hope, for her sake, that this was the last time he ever saw her. She shook her head.

"I will bring them everything they need. Everything."

Eighteen

Were they so stupid that they thought she kept all of her jewels in her bedroom for easy access? May shook her head in disgust. Of course the shorter one was clearly of a class that would know nothing about jewels, nor how things were done in the upper classes, and Delisle was French. Perhaps French ladies did things differently, or more likely he had a low opinion of the intelligence of English women. Her family's jewels, the pieces that had descended in the van Hoffen line, were kept in a safe at her bank in London, for there was little chance one would use them in the country. Only the simplest of pieces were kept at Lark House.

But she would have said anything to ensure that they kept Etienne alive, and if the promise of jewels and gold would do it, then she would promise, and then try to figure out what to do. It had been the only chance she had seen to keep the man she loved more than life itself alive.

May's hands trembled as she filled a silk sack, one that usually held her night rail when she traveled, with all of the gold from her strongbox in the library. She had carried the metal cask upstairs with her to her room when she came in, and now had it spilled over her bed, papers everywhere.

She flinched every time the coins clinked together. If there was one thing she could not afford tonight, it was Hannah asking questions. Although her abigail was fiercely loyal to her, she was also imperious on occasion and curious. May would never be able to explain any of this: blood on her night rail, the strong-box out, her filling a sack with gold . . . none of it!

Her hands shook as the realization hit her anew; they would kill Etienne. Unless she got them enough gold and gems, they would kill . . . She paused. The dark room was quiet, and she could almost hear her own heart pounding, the blood rushing through her veins at an accelerated rate. Would it make any difference at all whether she brought them jewels? Could they afford to let him live? Or her, for that matter?

She slumped down on the floor by the bed, a deep sob clogging her throat. That was why Etienne was pleading with her to stay inside. He knew her life was forfeit along with his own the minute she gave them what they wanted. They had no intention of letting either of them go. And so Etienne had made up that ridiculous code to tell her to "stay" in safety once she was in Lark House. Did he really think that she would lock herself in and wait, knowing those criminals were going to kill him?

No! She arose, her fists clenched around the silken sack. She had defeated Dempster, and she would find a way to defeat them.

Frantically she searched the room for something else to weight the bag with, for they must be dazzled by the haul. If they were as greedy as she thought they were, there might be some hope in that cupidity. She bethought herself of her mother's extensive collection. Yes, that would do!

She tore off her bloody night rail and stuffed it under her bed. It would not do to frighten Hannah. If she came in for something in the night and found her mistress's night rail on the floor with blood on it . . . well, May did not want to be responsible for what would happen. The poor woman would scream the house down. It was vital to her plan, and to Etienne's safety, that no one raise the alarm, or at least not too early. Swiftly and silently she slipped her breeches on and pulled the cambric shirt she always wore with it over her head and tucked it in, pushed her feet into her riding boots, then donned another heavy cloak—an old one that had belonged to her father and that she kept in her wardrobe—over the outfit. She slipped down the hall to her mother's room and spilled the contents of Maisie's jewel case into the blue silk sack and tied the top, letting some of the sparkling necklaces dangle out just a little to dazzle greedy eyes, then slipped down the stairs, and after one more stop, out the doors of the terrace.

The grass was slippery with dew, sparkling like jewels in the brilliant light of the rising moon. She ran down the slope, and then stopped to catch her breath. In the distance was the copse of trees, and she realized that if she was not careful, the man Etienne called Delisle would just shoot her as she approached. After all, they could then get the jewels from her dead fingers. Maybe they had already killed Etienne!

She clutched the bag to her breast. No! They would not do that until they were sure of her, until they knew she was coming back. And surely they would not risk shooting her until they knew what was in the sack.

They could not be so stupid that they would assume her compliance, could they? After all, she was no use to them dead, and she would have no reason to go along with them if *Etienne* was dead.

She walked on, wondering if she could circle and come up behind them, but no. There was no opportunity for that, because in the bright moonlight they would see her cross the barren expanse of lawn no matter which way she approached them from.

She would have to brazen this out, and hope her plan worked. It was their only chance. She trembled inside with fear, for Etienne and for herself, but she would not cower in the house while he died! She had defeated Dempster, had she not? Etienne thought she was brave; she must hold on to that. And after all, she concluded, what was courage but acting in the face of her fear, despite the trembling in her body and the clenching of her stomach?

Swallowing back the terror that threatened to leave her light-headed, she walked across the lawn. It was a long way on foot, and she searched the dark edge of the woods with frantic eyes the whole time. She couldn't see them. Had they gone? Had they killed Etienne, and waited to ambush her?

But no. As she got closer, she could make out the glare of Etienne's white shirt—he did not have a coat on—and then the pale faces of the men. She had to play her part just right, for never had so much been resting on her ability to conceal her true self.

She widened her eyes and swallowed hard as she approached Delisle and his friend and their captive. She dared not look into Etienne's eyes, or she would crumble. It was enough for now that he was alive, even though the sight of his blood trickling down and staining his shirt was enough to drive her to the edge of insanity.

"I . . . I brought it," she said, her voice trembling in the night quiet. "Everything I could find. G-gold from the strongbox, all of my jewels, and . . . and I emptied all of my mother's jewelry box into the bag, see?"

She held out the bag in her left hand and the moonlight sparkled off one particularly fabulous necklace. The red and white stones glittered and she saw Delisle's cold gray eyes fasten on it.

"Bring it to me," he hissed.

"How . . . oh." She sobbed, clutching the bag back to her breast. "How do I know you will let him go? Will you swear, on your honor, that you will let him go?"

Impatiently, he gestured into the air. "Yes, yes! I swear! Now bring it to me, or we will slit his throat and you will watch him die!"

"No!" she cried, staring with desperate eyes at Delisle. "Your friend must take the knife away from Etienne's throat. I will give it only to him. After all, you might intend to take it and kill us all, your friend included! I have heard there is no honor among thieves, and you do not strike me as the kind of man who would be willing to share a hoard such as I have brought you, tens of thousands of pounds worth of gems, with anyone!"

The other man glanced over at Delisle and frowned. " 'Ere, whot she says is right. Never did trust you Frenchies, an' you, my fine friend, you'd as soon slit your muvver's throat as look at 'er. So I'll take the jools!"

"Jem, you fool," Delisle muttered, impatiently.

"This is no time to argue! She is just trying to plant doubts in your mind about me. We have come this far, my partner, *trust* me."

That apparently was too much for the Englishman, and he released Etienne and lunged at May, trying to grab the bag of jewels, but she had calculated the distance at which she stood carefully, and once she saw the movement, she heaved the bag with all her might at his head. It hit him and he staggered back. Etienne had made the most of his precious seconds of freedom to tackle Delisle, who did not expect the threat to come from that direction. They fell to the ground and grappled.

"Oh no," May screamed, but Jem had only been momentarily routed, and with an angry grunt like a bull, he ran at her again. She drew the pistol she had secreted in the waistband of her breeches and fired at him, winging him in one shoulder. He fell to the ground with a cry of pain, and the two Frenchmen, rolling in the wet grass, paused.

Etienne had the other man pinned, but Delisle was not defeated, and swiftly used the advantage of those seconds to crack Etienne with the butt of the gun he still held. When May saw him do that, a rage so powerful it shook her to the core overtook her.

"No!" She raced forward and kicked the Frenchman's arm, and the pistol flew into the air.

Etienne, stunned but not beaten, flung himself on his antagonist again and shouted, "It is over, Delisle, it is over!"

"Damn right it's over! All of ye, on yer feet!"

May whirled around, and was never so glad to see anyone in her life as she was to see Bill Connors, followed by John Groom and Zach, the little stable boy.

Bill and John must have arrived home sometime that night! Bill rushed forward and grabbed Delisle, while John grasped Etienne in a tight grip. Zach rescued the pistol from the grass and held it on the recumbent figure of Jem Foster, who moaned and whimpered, holding his useless arm.

"Let him go, John," May cried, alarmed at how pale Etienne had become. "He is not one of them!"

"That's the gent what's bin livin' in the little house in the woods," Zach cried, proud of his—for once—superior knowledge over John, who lorded it over the small boy. "He's the one the mistress 'as bin visitin'."

The gunfire resounding in the clear, still night air had brought Stainer, two footmen, and Hannah running, and they all heard Zach and gazed at Etienne. The two footmen exchanged knowing looks at the boy's innocent revelation, and even Hannah looked shocked as she gazed at the young Frenchman.

"Those are clothes from the attic trunk," she blurted out. "I recognize those blue breeches as the ones Lady van Hoffen had me put up there after the fellow who owned them left." The abigail looked from Etienne to May and back again, a puzzled expression on her honest face.

May felt a flush burn into her cheeks. *No better than she should be.* She could hear the unsaid words, could feel the sweep of opinion. It was what she had guarded against her whole life, but now her actions in protecting Etienne would ruin her. *Just like her mother after all.* No one would ever say it, but they would whisper it. Regardless of the fact that it was her own staff that was witness to this debacle, in days—hours!—it would be through the county that she had secreted a man in her folly and given him clothes from one of her mother's paramours, and she would be ruined, her reputation in shreds. All her dreams for living at Lark House and doing good for the children, the school, all would be for naught, because no one would dare consort with a young lady of ill repute.

Etienne moved forward, his chin raised, his mien noble even though his shirt was bloody and grass-stained and his hair tousled. "I am Lord Etienne Roulant Delafont, cousin and heir presumptive to the Marquess of Sedgely." He put his arm around May's shoulders, and she sagged against him, grateful for his support. "Come, my love, they will need to know soon."

At the unaccustomed endearment she gazed up sharply into his eyes. What was he doing? What game was he playing? Mrs. Connors and two chambermaids ran down the lawn and joined the small crowd. One of the little maids gasped at the sight of the gentleman with his arms around the mistress in such a bold way.

He looked down into her eyes with a soft tenderness that made May weak with love. She reached up and touched his cheek, grateful just that he was alive. If her reputation was ruined she would live the rest of her life in seclusion, and not count the cost too high for the life of her beloved.

But Etienne squeezed her, smiled down into her eyes, and spoke again. "I am going to tell them. They should all know." He gazed at the servants, collecting every one of their attentions as he surveyed them all. "Your mistress and I met in London last spring. Lady May was concealing me in her folly, for I was in grave danger from these two. I was doing secret work for the government, and so could not reveal myself, but now it can be told. We are in love and will be married as soon as possible.''

LADY MAY'S FOLLY

the government, and so could not foment unrest. But
when it can be done. We are in love and will be married
as soon as possible.

Nineteen

Pearl gray dawn peered into the rose and yellow
breakfast parlor through lace curtains. For all the
world like an old married couple, Etienne and May
sat in silence at the round oak table, sipping steaming
cups of coffee.

Their long ordeal was finally over, and now others
would take care of the details. Bill Connors had en-
listed the help of a couple of the sturdier cottagers
from the home farm to round up the miscreants and
take them to the village constable and to justice. May
had told them about the third man, Dempster, who
was to be found in the woods near the folly, and said
to tell the constable he could visit later for the whole
story. She had no idea what to tell the man about
Delisle and his cohort, but maybe Etienne would have
an idea of what to say that would not bring himself
into it. She was too tired to think.

John Groom and Zach had been sent out to find
Cassie and Théron, though Etienne doubted whether
Théron would allow himself to be taken docilely to a
strange stable without his owner present. He was in
no shape to assist, though, and had barely been able
to limp up to the house. He had gazed at Lark House
in silent amazement as they approached it, not having
realized before how large a home May owned.

One moment of levity occurred. As they walked away from the copse, Etienne had glanced back at the sparkling jewels in the grass, and expressed concern that they should be gathered up and returned to a safe. May had sent a sideways glance his way. "I really don't give a fig if they lie there until Christmas," she said. "The gold yes, but the jewels, no."

"What? But they are your mother's jewels! So very valuable."

"Paste. All paste. A hundred pounds worth of glass."

Etienne had laughed, though his face was still lined with weariness and pain. "So the two quarreled over a collection of glass gemstones! How fitting." They had walked up to the house arm in arm.

The household being awake anyway, May had asked Mrs. Connors if she felt up to making a restorative meal for his lordship and herself. Of course the woman had said yes. She had eyed Etienne with questioning eyes at first, but after Hannah whispered something to her, something about his role in saving May's life in the London episode, for she had recognized the man's name as soon as he had introduced himself, the woman looked more kindly on him, and created a breakfast fit for royalty.

And so they had eaten, and May had allowed no one else but herself to see to the precious task of bandaging Etienne's poor throat. She eyed him over the rim of her coffee cup, and then finally set it down. He was gazing off into the distance with a sad look in his brown eyes. What irony, she thought, that she must now submit to a false engagement to a man she would marry, if he would really have her. The *only* man she would marry, she corrected herself.

"How could you say that?" she muttered, her voice echoing strangely in the silent room. It was disorienting seeing Etienne in her home, in the prosaic surrounding of her pretty rose and yellow morning room. "How could you say we are engaged when it is not true?"

"I only thought of your reputation, little one. So much better to be secreting your heroic fiancé than some escaped murderer." His voice was bitter, but he added a sad smile to soften his words.

She ignored the last part. "My reputation? What is going to happen to my reputation when they find out it is all a sham? When we do not marry?"

"We will think of something. These people love you," he said. "I saw it in the satisfaction that man, Connors, took in taking your attacker to justice. The way the small boy claimed the right to bring back your beautiful mare. The way your maid and cook whispered, and agreed to wait on me when they realized I had some small hand in helping you last spring. If they think I have cruelly used you, they will rally around you and save you from public opinion."

But who will save me from my own heart, when you leave, she thought. That, though, was reflection for a quieter time, when she was alone with her thoughts. "You don't know anything about the English countryside," she said. "One word to the vicar, and I will be ruined anyway, for regardless of the reason, I still secreted you in my folly and visited you for long hours, alone." As she said it, she realized that it sounded like she blamed him, but she didn't.

He came around the table and knelt in front of her, taking her hands in his. For one wild moment she wondered if he would really propose to her now. What would she say? How would she react, knowing he married her only to save her reputation? She would say yes, of course! She would have him on any terms.

His brown eyes met her blue ones. "I am still a wanted man, or I would truly ask you to marry, just to save your reputation. But I tried to kill my cousin. I tried to murder him for the title and for the money! And I will tell the constable the truth, when they come to speak to us. I must be honest, finally."

A cold hand of fear clutched at her heart. "No," she cried, turning her face away, refusing to gaze in honest brown eyes that swore he was telling the truth. "I do not believe you ever did any such thing. I will not believe it!" She tried to ignore the pain of his words, his *first* words, that if he could he would marry her "just to save her reputation." She had thought it would be enough, when it occurred to her that he might do just that thing, but it wouldn't. *Oh, Etienne,* she thought. *Not for love? You could not marry me for love?*

"I will not believe it of you!" she repeated, pushing away the pain. "You are not capable of plotting cold-blooded murder."

"It is true," he said, squeezing her hands and pressing them to his heart.

"I will never believe you could be so despicable."

"Believe it, for it is true." He dropped her hands and rose, pacing to the window and gazing out over the sunny landscape. "I will tell you all. It is the only way you will believe me, it seems, for you have a too-good opinion of my worth, and as much as it hurts, I would have you know the truth of me. I fear you have made me into a paper hero, little one, and as much as it hurts to do it, I will shred that flimsy thing, for you must know the truth."

As the morning sun rose, Etienne first told her about how the present marquess's great-grandfather had a brother who moved to France, married a Frenchwoman, and bore sons, who had sons, who had sons, to the present—his—generation. The male line had not done so well in England, so that was how he, Etienne Roulant Delafont, came to be the present marquess's heir presumptive.

Always he had known he was related to the English titular head of the family, but had not been aware that in the intervening years other closer claimants had died, bearing only daughters or no progeny at all. And so he was the heir without even knowing it.

Meanwhile, he got himself in a little trouble, he said with a wry smile. Paris, in the days following the end of the war, had been a boisterous and rowdy place, and Englishmen arrived in flocks, looking for merriment and debauchery. Delisle ran a gambling house, and Etienne, looking to make a little money from the so-willing English, had taken to gambling. He had always been very good at games of chance, spectacularly good, in fact. But in one memorable night—or perhaps it was two nights, he had not slept, that is all he knew—he had lost a fortune that had been advanced to him by Delisle.

Etienne frowned. "I cannot believe I had such bad luck! I have always been skilled and lucky . . . a very good combination at the games of chance."

"How could you have such a prolonged losing streak if it was pure luck?" May asked. They sat talking over yet another cup of steaming coffee. "You would think that at least you would break even."

Running his thumb around the rim of the china cup, Etienne slowly shook his head. Then his dark eyes widened. "I wonder . . . but how?"

"What is it? What has occurred to you?"

"Always I have wondered why Delisle, who is greedy and devious in the extreme, why he was so philosophical about the horrendous amount I owed him. I will tell you the rest of the story, and then you tell me if something does not seem right."

Delisle learned by chance, Etienne continued, that he, Etienne Delafont, was the heir presumptive to Baxter Delafont, the English Marquess of Sedgely, and that Sedgely was actually traveling through France at that very moment, and had stopped in Paris for a few weeks.

Fabulously wealthy was the marquess, and yet Etienne had nothing. Was that right? Delisle whispered to Etienne. The Englishman had everything, and he, a Delafont, too, had been left by the war with nothing. He should kill the Englishman and inherit all that lovely money, and the title, too!

Etienne had agreed.

"How could you agree to it? How could you go along with such a terrible plot?" May whispered. The tale seemed so incongruous, so dark and terrible and yet told in such bright, sunny surroundings. She stared at the man before her, the man she would have sworn she knew as well as she knew anyone on earth. But what did she really know about him, other than what he had chosen to tell her? Had he withheld the awful truth so she would continue helping him in his desperate circumstance?

Etienne glanced away from the window toward May.

"Ah, now you begin to see how unworthy I am of your sweetness, and your giving."

There was a dark and terrible sadness in Etienne's brown eyes. His face was haggard and shadowed by beard stubble and the bandage around his throat and across his brow, where the butt of the gun had struck him, made him look so very vulnerable. Even now, even as he told her this awful story, she wanted to take him into her arms and nestle him against her heart. What did that say about her, that she would take an admitted criminal to her bosom? She turned away, afraid, suddenly, that her love was misplaced, and yet irrecoverable.

She could not even bear to look at him, Etienne thought. And so she should not. He would tell her everything, for he thought that she was beginning to love him a little, and he must destroy that sweet feeling so she could continue her life without him and be happy with some other man, someone who deserved her. There was no one alive who did, but perhaps she would find someone to love who at least was not such a villain.

"I had done a lot of things during the war. I fought against Napoleon's men with the Belgians for a while. But never had I killed a man in cold blood. My first attempt in France to kill my cousin was weak, and I could not stomach the job. I abandoned it. And then I thought that if I could find my way into the marquess's room, I could steal some money and go away, to Italy, or even to England. Always I have had a soft spot for England." He gazed at May. And never more than that moment, he thought. Never more than when his very heart was engaged to a woman who represented to him the best England had to offer.

Courage, fortitude, inner strength tempered by a sweetness so vivid it pierced his heart like an arrow shot true from Cupid's bow; all of that she had and was. And yet she was not for him.

He roused himself and continued, pausing only as a footman came in to clear the table and bring in more coffee, at May's request. He took a cup and drained it, then continued his tale.

"But he carried nothing of value, and I left the room upon being discovered by the marquess and his paramour. Delisle threatened me for the first time. If I did not deliver the money I owed him, even though I had been cheated at the tables and he knew it, I would be the one to die. And I had thought him a friend!"

May frowned and glared down at her cup, and pinched up a pleat of the lace tablecloth. If Delisle knew Etienne had been cheated at the table, who better could have arranged it than himself? And he was the one from whom the first knowledge of Etienne's inheritance had come. What was the connection there?

"And so I assaulted my good cousin again," Etienne continued, pacing away from the table and staring out the window once more. "On the packet from Calais, while it waited in dock to cross to England, I . . . how do you English say it? I 'coshed' him. I was supposed to then finish him with a knife, slit his throat—you see the irony of this, eh?" he said, touching the bandage at his throat. May glanced at him, and the pain in her eyes made his pitiful joke fall flat. She would turn from him in hatred before he was through with his story, and yet he must tell her all.

He must be the assassin of any gentle feelings she cherished for him in her generous heart.

"I was to slit his throat and leave him to bleed to death, alone, on the deck of the ship." He spoke in a monotone, remembering the dark of the night, the wet deck, the tang of the salt air, and himself, standing over the big man's body. "I could not do it," he whispered. "I did not even know him. Was he a good man? What was his life like? I could not kill him so coldly. And so I raised the alarm so he would be found, and escaped, after I was sure people came to his aid."

May glanced up at him with a puzzled expression. Her blue eyes were a deeper color, he thought, gazing into them. She was tired, but so rigidly she held herself, so upright, his little English miss. No, not his. He wanted to sweep her hair out of her eyes and kiss her, but he maintained the absolute control he had promised himself.

"You called the watch to save his life," she said, pensively. "So why did you come to England?"

"I had to escape Delisle, and as I was in Calais, it was easiest to stow away aboard a packet to England. What I did not know was that Delisle had his English toady watching me. He reported everything, and they caught up with me in England. I was still the English marquess's heir, they said. *They* would kill him, *I* would inherit, and they would take an additional ten thousand pounds, or they would incriminate me. And I had no defense, for I was guilty of trying to kill him, no? And Delisle had my signed note to pay him a great deal of money. It would not look good for me."

May frowned. "So the attack . . . the first one in England. Was that you?"

"No, it was Delisle and Jem Foster. I . . . I had been

following them, afraid of what they would do, and I stepped in at the convenient time and chased them off. I made a very poor assassin, you see. I wondered if I should stay in London. Perhaps as heir I was entitled to something; I did not know about English law. But Delisle and Jem decided they were on their own, but that it was still worth their while to kill the marquess. Once I had inherited—for they did not think I would be able to resist coming forward with my claim—then they would step in and extort money from me.

"Or they would abduct the marquess and hold him for ransom. I had met the marquess by that time, and had no wish to see him dead. And I had met . . . Emily. I knew that I should leave London . . . England, in fact . . . before I got caught, but I stayed."

Because of his attraction to Emily, May thought. Always it came back to Emily. As much as she loved the woman, who had been a good friend to her, a searing jealousy still pierced her. Emily was everything she was not; older, voluptuous, experienced, beautiful . . . and married. Perfect for an affair.

"Who would have thought Lord Sedgely would have such a hard head." Etienne chuckled dryly. "And thank God, or I would consider myself a murderer indeed and not just in intent, even if it was not I who struck the blow. Delisle and Jem attacked the marquess directly in front of Lady Sedgely's home, the fools, and just then her carriage came, and her coachman chased them off just as they had been trying to drag him into the shadows. Thank God," he said, fervently. "And thank God my Lord Sedgely is such a giant, for he was heavier than they expected, I think.

"Anyway, when I found out what was going on from an informant—it was the night of the Duc de LaCoursiere's masquerade—that they were going to kill him and then come to me when I inherited, I sent them a message. I was leaving. It was my best chance of ensuring the marquess's safety. I was disappearing for good, and if they killed the marquess, they would get nothing for it. And that is what I did, after a memorable side trip to find you, little one."

The endearment, which had started out irritating her endlessly and now sounded like the sweetest words in the English language, almost undid her, but she had to stay strong. There was a growing seed of hope planted within her, but there was more still to learn.

"And what did you do while on the run from them?"

Etienne shook his head. "You do not want to know all, little one."

"Were you"—she held her breath—"were you stealing or . . . or anything."

"I am not a common thief," he said, drawing himself up. Then his shoulders slumped. "Of whom am I speaking? I am not a thief, I am a filthy murderer."

"What did you do? What have you been doing the last six months?"

"I have been staying one step ahead of Delisle and Jem. I can only suppose they had hoped to take vengeance on me for not falling in with their plan, or perhaps they had hope, still, that I could be forced to go along. But I escaped them. Many lovely Englishwomen have sheltered me," he said, "nice women who fed and sheltered me out of the goodness of their hearts."

And the lust of their bodies, May thought wryly, knowing Etienne's effect on any woman with eyes to see and a heart that still pumped red blood. Even haggard, wounded, tired, he was more man than most Englishwomen would know how to resist.

"But finally they caught me . . . in bed, of all places. That is how I got wounded. Delisle is nasty, that one, and good with a knife. I only made it away because of the brave heart of Théron, noble beast that he is. They had never been fooled by my supposed drowning in the channel and had almost caught me more than once. This time they did."

"Seems like a lot of trouble to go to on their part," May said.

"Ah, but the payment would be rich, if I inherited, for they would have the blackmail victim for life. And then I made Delisle angry by refusing him. He does not like to be refused anything. But here my story ends. I was in your folly dying, and you found me and brought me back to life. I deserved to die. I tried to kill the marquess, and should have hung on the gallows. But I do not want to die. I like life and all it has to offer. So I have a decision to make now that Delisle and Jem are caught. Either I will be brave, and confess all, and will go to the gallows, or I will escape yet again. I will go to France."

"Do you . . . do you have someone there? Do you have a home, friends . . . a . . . a woman?"

He did not look into her eyes. "There is only one woman in my heart ever, but alas, I can never have her."

May hung her head. It was as she suspected. A married woman had captured his heart, at some time past, and he was not free to love someone like her. But still, she did love *him,* and she would do what was right.

"I won't let you live under a shadow, Etienne. You saved my life again; you threw yourself on Delisle when he was ready to shoot me."

"No, little one. You saved mine. Yet again."

She sighed and crossed her arms over her modest bosom. "Well, whoever saved whomever, I want your name cleared."

"And why do I deserve that, little one? Why do I deserve your so-gallant defense?"

She stood and crossed the room to stand at the window with him. She longed to touch him, to hold him, but kept herself rigidly separate from him. "You asked me what I thought of the whole story. I think that Delisle set you up from the beginning. I think it was he who made you lose at the tables, so you would be in his debt. It seems to me that he must already have known that you were Lord Sedgely's heir, and concocted that plan to benefit himself from it."

Etienne sighed and nodded. "It is what I believe now, too. I always knew that I must have been cheated to lose so consistently, but I put it down to a crooked dealer, or shady player. But who better to fix the games than the owner of the gambling club?"

"And then he played on any feeling of misuse you might feel."

Shame-faced, Etienne admitted the justice of her words. "He did do that. He said how wrong it was that I should be a beggar while the English branch of my family was wealthy beyond belief. But still, it does not excuse what I did."

"Maybe not," May said, softly. She reached out and stroked his arm. "But in the end you could not do it.

Just as I always said, you are too fine a man to ever do something so terrible. We are not going to tell the constable about your connection with Delisle and Jem. You and I are going to Surrey. You are going to beg your cousin's forgiveness for your foolishness, and he is going to forgive you, because after all, you did not really try to kill him. In fact you saved his life!"

"But . . ."

"No 'buts' Etienne! We are doing this," she said. "You are going to be free of this burden. Lord Sedgely is going to exonerate you of any wrongdoing because you are going to tell him your story, exactly as you told it to me."

Twenty

May was adamant. By the end of that day she had persuaded Isabel Naunce—very much against her brother's wishes—to stay with her and lend her countenance until she and Etienne could travel down to Surrey. She told everyone that they were going, now that the danger to Etienne was over, down to visit his cousin before they wed. It was the truth, after all, she argued with Etienne, or at least partly the truth.

Then she called in the doctor, who treated Etienne's wounds properly and gave them an ointment that would surely heal the wound much better than an unguent meant for a horse. It began to work quickly, taking away the festering look by the next day and staunching the ugly gray pus that had infected the area.

She was tireless, May was, he thought, watching her over the two days before they started their journey. Lark House was an efficiently run household, he thought, because of her, because she expected everyone to do their jobs well, but at the same time was not rigid in her expectations, allowing them to do those jobs in their own way. He did not think she realized the depth of devotion she had inspired in her people. Her energy extended beyond their own preparations for their trip to Surrey. She even thought of the people in the village to whom she offered charity, though she did not call it charity.

She had a long meeting with Bill Connors, planning what was to be done for a family in the village named Johnson. Since she did not have a steward anymore, she was going to hire, she said, Mr. Johnson, so that he would not need to work twelve hours a day any longer for his growing family. He would take the cottage evacuated by Crandall, the old steward, and live on Lark House land.

Others in the village she committed to the care of Mrs. Naunce, who though wary of May at first, seemed to come more to appreciate all of her sterling qualities over the two days. She would take care of the others, she told May, and gladly. And the harvest festival would go on as planned in just a few weeks now. They would all work together.

With a fatalism he had never allowed himself to feel before, Etienne thought that it was ridiculous to make this trip, but he did not have sufficient energy to counteract May. She was a whirlwind of activity. But the staff willingly went along with any request she made. There was nothing they would not do for her. He had the feeling they were all grateful to her for not being her mother. Maisie van Hoffen had had a reputation for shaming her staff so they could hardly hold their heads up among their fellow serving class. According to May, she was mending her ways now, but it was too late for her in this county. Always she would be branded by her past actions, though no stain of the mother's sordid past had ever touched May.

And he had come so close to spoiling her newfound position in the community by his mere presence. It was still going to be a matter for her of brazening it out, when it was discovered that she would not be marrying him after all. But she would do well without him there. Her household loved and respected her, and they would support whatever story she decided to tell to explain his defection.

For he would not be coming back to Lark House, no matter what May thought. She did not seem to be thinking that far ahead, but from some things she said she obviously assumed he would be coming back to Lark House to convalesce. This came out in connection to his horse. Surprisingly, it was Zach, the young stable boy, who eventually found Théron and was able to lead him back. Cassie had come back on her own just hours after the confrontation at the edge of the woods, but his stallion finally appeared on the very morning Etienne and May were to leave. He was exhausted, and Etienne was concerned for his old friend until he saw how the horse had taken to the lad, who had a way with horseflesh that must have been bred in the bones.

May said, "We'll leave him here to recover until we come back. By then he will be back to his proper strength."

Etienne did not say what was in his heart, that he would never see Lark House again. It was too early for that particular argument.

And so they were off to Surrey. There was no way to dissuade May from her course of action. He should have just slipped away in the night, but he owed her so much, more than he would ever be able to repay, and he would finally face down the truth. He saw no reason in the world why Lord Sedgely would not just kill him outright, especially in light of an episode that Etienne was forced to reveal to May. It was not one of his finest hours, but he wearily decided that he would follow the English adage of "in for a penny in for a pound."

They left on a fine fall morning, when the frost was still on the ground, sparkling in the low-rising sun. May had insisted that he purchase new garments, though he did not have any money. The only thing he had of any value was Théron, and his horse was his friend more than his property. But he owed her a debt. It was composed of more than mere money, and so it was fitting that when he left May behind, he would leave her his steed. Théron would have a good home with his new girlfriend, Cassie, and his private thought was that May perhaps already had the beginning of a champion stud line in the pair. It would hurt more than he cared to think to leave his horse behind, but there was no one else in the world who would care for him as well as May.

As they rode that first morning, the swaying and jolting of the enclosed carriage settling as they got off the country roads onto the better traveled highways, he decided it was the right time to tell her the whole truth of his dealings with Lord Sedgely. Hannah sat with them, but dozed, her chin touching her chest and her head bobbing with the sway of the vehicle.

He looked over at May and took her hand, gazing down at the tan gloves she wore with a brown carriage dress and gold spencer. "You know, the marquess, he may refuse to see me."

"Nonsense! You did not have a good chance to get to know him, but in the time I spent in their town house, while I was waiting to sort everything out regarding my mother, I found that beneath that steely exterior, he is really rather a lamb!"

Etienne quirked her a comical look of horror, and she laughed and squeezed his hand. There was some strong emotion in her pretty blue eyes, but he had lately learned humility, and did not think it was love. She had treated him, the last couple of days, like a brother, and he accepted that she had affection for him, but not the love of a lover. He had been able to arouse her body, but skill did not equal love.

"Regardless, Lord Sedgely has every reason for hating me. I . . . I fear I prolonged his separation from his wife with . . . with my lies."

He saw a coolness settle over her features and feared it would turn to ice soon, but there was nothing for it but to tell her the whole truth. He took a deep breath, and prepared himself for her censure. "You see, I had lost my desire to kill the marquess, but still, I think, I harbored the envy of his position, of his money. He was . . . is my kinsman, but has all the wealth and prestige I have never had and never will attain. The morning after I chased Delisle and Jem off from the marquess, I visited him, and met fair Emily. She is what I have always thought of as the ideal in womanhood, plump and pretty, dark hair, dark eyes . . . older than I, and . . . well, motherly, but not, if you know what I mean . . ."

May held herself rigid as she listened to him extol the virtues of the woman they were about to visit.

"I wanted her, I will not deny that. Always I have conducted affairs with older women, and I found her irresistible. I say this not to excuse myself, but to explain." He glanced over at May, noting the glacial blue of her eyes, and then continued. "I pursued her. But there came a time when I knew that she was vacillating between her husband and myself, or at least

I felt she was. I wanted to tip the scales, and so I took a chance. Lord Sedgely had seen Emily and me go into the conservatory of the Duttons' home, and his wife had looked very, very guilty. We . . . well, we kissed, there, and talked for at least an hour. But nothing more. She would let me go no further, and even then I think I knew that it was still her husband in her heart and mind that kept her from engaging in an *affaire* with me. I went to Lord Sedgely's house the next morning and told him we had made love there.''

Her heart threatened to rend in two, May thought, holding back tears with difficulty. So that was it. As she had suspected, Emily was the woman, the married woman, to whom his heart was promised. It hurt badly, and it made what she was doing and where she was going all that much more difficult, but she was doing this for Etienne, and she must keep his welfare firmly in mind, rather than dwell upon her breaking heart.

He required no answer to his story, and May could not think of a word to say. So that was some of what had gone on among the three the previous spring. She had been so caught up in her own affairs, and her fear of Dempster and his devious plans, that she had known little of what actually occurred. It was clear to her now, though, that Etienne still cherished love in his heart for Emily. She must think of *him*, and how it was going to hurt, seeing her there in her home and happy, large with her husband's child.

They stopped for the night at a small inn, retired early to their separate chambers, and then started off again early. The rest of the trip passed in near silence.

Brockwith was a large, pleasant Palladian home set in a lovely valley in Surrey. May had not sent word ahead that they would be coming for a number of reasons, and so when they pulled up at the front portico of the house, they were surprised to see the doors flung open. Etienne and May exchanged looks as a harried butler came out on the steps, glanced down at them, and then hurried back into the manor.

Etienne descended to the ground and was reaching in to help May out when Dodo Delafont came storming out screeching over her shoulder, "What do you mean it is not the doctor, Cromby! Who else would it be?"

Her expression when she looked and found Etienne and May there was almost comical, her thin mouth an O of surprise.

"What is wrong, Dodo?" May asked, trotting up the steps and giving the older woman a brief hug. Hannah followed her mistress up the steps and stood waiting a discreet distance away.

Dodo looked a little surprised, but said, "It's Emily! It is too early, but we think she has gone into labor! Baxter has gone for the doctor, and that is who I thought the carriage was."

She glanced down, saw Etienne, and froze. "What is he doing here?" she said, pointing with one shaky finger. "I thought he was dead! What is he doing here?"

"It is a very long story. May we come in?"

Etienne steeled himself to be tossed forcibly from the property; it was no better than he deserved. But Dodo gave him a puzzled look, then threw up her hands. "Come in, come in. This is no time to be quibbling."

It was a bad time to come, May thought as they followed the older woman into the mansion. She

glanced at Etienne's face, waiting to see his anxiety
on behalf of the woman he loved. This could not be
easy for him, being in the home where she was
brought to bed with the child she bore her husband.
But his face and attitude expressed no more than a
proper amount of worry on Emily's behalf. What a
good actor he was! And that was a good thing, for it
would not be proper for him to show his true feelings
in Emily's own home and in front of her family.

They awaited Lord Sedgely's return in a main floor
salon, done in ivory and gold, with lovely, delicate
Sheraton furniture. Dodo excused herself to return
to Emily, and though May wanted to go up to the
mother-to-be, she accepted the older woman's belief
that it was best if she waited.

"She is right, little one. Best to leave the poor
woman undisturbed. Why do we not walk in the garden while we await the marquess?"

May allowed him to lead her outside, leaving Hannah with her sewing in the salon. Brockwith was in a
valley with a long hill behind it, and a ridge of trees
along the top that tossed anxiously in the autumn
wind, brown and golden leaves tumbling across the
grass like a troupe of small acrobats. It was all very
lovely, but she still preferred her own home, Lark
House.

"You know," Etienne said, drawing her arm
through his as they walked through the garden of
bronze and gold chrysanthemums, "Lord Sedgely will
be within his rights to throw me from the property
rather than listen to what I have to say. And you know
that if he challenges me to a fight, I will not fight him.
I will allow him to do whatever honor demands of

him. I will take what punishment he deems just, for I have done him great and repeated injury."

May squeezed his arm and laid her cheek against his shoulder. "We *must* make him listen, Etienne. I know you were wrong, but there were other forces at work, and once he hears all . . . I think he is a fair man, even if he is not merciful."

"Just so you know I shall abide by whatever he says. If he wishes to turn me in to English law, I will go, I have decided. He was in danger, and it was all my fault."

They walked on in silence for a few minutes, then sat, by mutual agreement, on a small stone bench set in a shelter at one end of a reflecting pool. Their hands stayed twined and May thought how good, how right this felt to her. He was the husband of her heart, as he could never be the husband of her body. And so she would always think of him, as her lover, husband, most adored mate for life. But it was not the same for him. No, she did not have even any lingering hope of that.

She glanced up at him. He was gazing into the distance and absently stroking her hand with his thumb. "This must be so hard for you," she said.

"It is. I would not be here but for your insistence."

"I know," May said, her heart breaking at the tortured sound of his voice. "It . . . it must be so difficult to know the . . . the woman you love is . . . is . . ." Her voice choked and she could not continue.

He darted a glance at her and took a deep breath. "Yes? The woman I love is . . . ?"

"Etienne, I know how you feel about her. I know how much you love Emily . . . if it would help to talk . . . to . . ." She broke off again, her voice thick with emotion.

"What are you talking about?" Etienne said, watching a tear spill from the corner of her eye. Never had he seen his little one weep. Why now?

"Emily! It must be hard to know she is up there, bearing Baxter's child, in pain . . ." She broke off when she saw the look of mixed confusion and laughter on his face.

"My dear little one, what an imagination. Is that what you think, that I have been cherishing the *tendre* for the marchioness?"

Her blue eyes were clouded with confusion. "Well, yes. Haven't you?"

"No. I felt for her at one time passion, yes. And I like her. She is a very special woman, but not for me. I am glad the foolish marquess has mended his fences and is now to carry on the line. Emily deserves happiness, and as you once told me, she very much loves her husband, I think."

May puzzled through all of the misconceptions she had been carrying. She could not possibly mistake his calm tone, his detached demeanor. She almost missed his whispered, "No, she is not the woman with whom I have fallen in love."

But she did hear it. "Who is, then?"

"Can you not guess?" He shook his head and gazed down at her, a trace of a smile on his lips. "I have been more circumspect than I would have thought, then."

Her heart throbbed erratically. What did he mean? Who was the woman? She felt the dawn of a trembling hope, but was too afraid to let it grow. "Who are you in love with, then?"

He shook his head, and was about to answer, when Baxter Delafont came striding around the corner of the manor house. "I heard you were here. What do you want?"

He did not say a word to May, but she stepped between the two men, for Etienne had risen at Baxter's approach. The marquess's lean, grim face was set in angry lines, but his black eyes were shadowed with fear and pain, and considering Emily's dangerous state, May tried to be gentle, despite the harshness of his words.

"Please, my lord, I know this is not the ideal time, but will you listen to what Etienne has to say? Without anger?"

He looked up at a third floor window and clenched his fists. May guessed that was where Emily lay, and she put out one hand and laid it on his powerful arm. She felt his muscles tense.

"They sent me away," he said, dark anguish in his voice. "They say I am agitating Emily with my pacing, but she is in pain! It is too early! Something is not right. I can't lose her; I can't." He stifled a sob and his face was twisted into an ugly grimace.

"I understand how you feel, my lord," Etienne said, gently. "I, too, have suffered those pains."

The marquess sent him a dark look of utter disgust, his lip pulled back in a snarl of hatred.

"Not for Emily . . . Lady Sedgely!" Etienne hastily said. "But I have recently watched the woman I love in danger, and it is the worst feeling I think I have ever suffered. I am truly sorry for your anguish. I will pray for her recovery, for your sake. God will be merciful."

May stared at him, but he would not meet her eyes.

Whom did he mean? Was he just cozening Baxter with false sympathy? But no, she knew him too well now. His voice held remembered pain, and great sympathy.

Baxter must have heard it, too, because after a long minute when he stared at Etienne, and the younger man stood still and calm under his scrutiny, the marquess said, "Walk with me. I will listen to you, but I swear if I do not like what I hear, I reserve the right to beat you to a *pulp* afterward."

Etienne gave May a look and shrugged. *I told you so,* he mouthed to her. Then he said, "It is a deal, my lord."

The two men walked away.

Twenty-one

May paced anxiously in the large central gallery that the great hall opened into. Baxter and Etienne had been gone for hours! In that time Emily had not yet borne her child or children, and her labor continued.

At first May had been calm and had taken tea; she had even read the newspaper. But as the hours went, she began to worry. The marquess was not noted for his even temper, and was, in fact, accounted a dangerous man to cross. Emily once told May that she knew her husband struggled every day with his anger, but that it was a point of pride with him not to lose his temper, and never to show physical evidence of it, unless in a dangerous spot.

So she could hope that Etienne was still alive, at least. But where *were* they?

The front door opened and the two men came in at that moment, their heads bent together in conversation, and she let out a long sigh of relief. It could not have ended badly if they were still speaking. Just then a thudding sound on the steps into the hall from upstairs echoed, and all three looked up to see Dodo, as old as she was, fly down the steps. She looked around wildly and then flung herself at her nephew, her long arms going around his waist in a fierce embrace. She was incoherent, but to everyone's amazement the woman some condemned as taciturn and others as just cold, kissed her nephew right in front of May and Etienne.

The marquess held her away from him and stared into her eyes. "Is she all right? Is my Emily all right?"

"All right? She is radiant, perfect! You are a father, Baxter. Two!" She wept and clung to her nephew, tears, streaming in rivulets, caught in the wrinkles on her cheeks and dripped onto his coat. Her hair was wild, pulled out of her normally tidy bun, but her expression was joyful. "A b-boy and a darling little g-girl!"

With an inarticulate yell of happiness Baxter raced for the stairs, taking them two at a time, followed closely by his galloping aunt.

"Two babies." May sighed happily. "What a happy day for them."

"Indeed," Etienne said. "And thank a merciful God all are well, and I am no longer the heir presumptive."

She turned and looked at him, noting the weariness on his face. "Did you sort out your differences, sir?" she asked, a note of tenderness in her voice. She wanted to gather him to her and ease his fatigue. He was limping, she had noticed, the wound still not healed up, although it was more quickly on the mend. But he still should not have been on his feet for so long, especially if they had been walking the whole time. She did not doubt that they had, as the marquess's anxiety for his wife would probably not allow him to rest for long.

"We did. I offered to stand still while he beat me

to a pulp or ran me through with his sword. I think that helped. And then I told him everything."

"Everything?"

"Everything," Etienne said, firmly. "And I apologized—for the lies I told, and for trying to kill him." He gave her a wry smile. "That took much on his part to forgive. But he finally said that in an odd way, I brought him and Emily back together, for she came to him out of concern for his injury, after Delisle coshed him. And so though he might deplore the method, he said, he could not argue with the outcome. Then he questioned me at length about my family, the little that is left of it: my sisters, me. I told him how my father died, a hero, struggling against the revolution's vicious campaign of hatred."

Eventually, after a meal, May and Etienne were invited up to see the new children, two pink squirming bundles with the grand titles of Sylvester Baxter Eggleton Delafont, Earl of Hartwick, and Lady Dianne Charlotte Eleanor Delafont. For a few minutes May sat and held in her arms the tiny Lady Dianne. Her heart throbbed with an odd, pulsing beat as she looked down at the tiny, perfect fingers and pudgy, wizened face. Mere hours old, the baby still had that red color of a newborn, but to May it was beautiful. She had never thought herself one for children, but somehow, with this brand-new life in her arms she thought she could certainly come to love them. Especially one of her own.

But that would never be.

She glanced up to find Etienne, holding the tiny Lord Sylvester in his arms, gazing steadily at her with an indescribable look in his tawny eyes. What a father he would make, she thought, and incredibly, tears

welled up in her eyes. How she would love to share
that with him! She blinked the tears away and surren-
dered the baby back to Baxter, who tenderly carried
the girl child over to her mother.

They had, of course, been invited to stay. Emily had
been a little weepy and clearly exhausted from her
ordeal, but she had insisted that she wanted her dear
friend May to stay at least overnight. Now that May
found the woman was not the object of Etienne's affections, it was much easier to smile at her and agree,
and remember the closeness they had shared. And
so, after a late supper and a little conversation with
Dodo, she retired to her room and allowed Hannah
to ready her for bed.

But May was restless. Nothing had been settled, and
so much that Etienne had said that day puzzled her.
There had not been a single moment alone to talk,
in a household with two new babies at the center of
the world.

Unable to sleep and unwilling to just lie in bed
awake all night, May crept down to the library, hoping
to find something to read that would be a soporific.
With a start, she saw a figure framed in the window
looking out at the waning moon. Was it Baxter? But
no, this figure was not quite so tall.

It was Etienne.

She squared her shoulders as if preparing to do
battle, and walked quietly to the center of the room.
It was time to find out what his true feeling were about
everything, because she was tired of guessing.

"Etienne," she whispered, very aware of her long
hair floating around her shoulders, and her flimsy
night rail under a soft challis wrap.

He turned and her breath caught at the tortured

look on his handsome, haggard face. "What is wrong?" She gasped, crossing the carpeted floor to him. She took his hands and stood staring up into his dark eyes.

"Nothing is wrong. Nothing. I will be leaving in the morning, unless you need me to escort you back to Kent." He pulled his hands out of her grasp and turned to gaze out the window again at the moon-touched landscape.

"Leaving? Why are you leaving?" she asked. But in her heart, she felt her questions were answered. He could not love her and be so willing to leave.

"I must go. We both know that."

She pushed his shoulder, forcing him around to look at her again. "I don't want you to go!"

"Do not make this harder for me, little one," he said, anguish staining his beautiful voice. He moved to take her in his arms and then stopped, letting his arms rest at his sides. "I must go. You may tell your people that I . . . that I died. That will surely preserve your honor, your reputation."

"Or . . ." She paused and looked up into his eyes still. She took a deep breath and said, "Or we could marry!"

He laughed, a mirthless sound in the dull quiet of the library. Her heart constricted as if he had stomped on it with one booted foot. If he could laugh at a proposal of marriage from her, it was the end and hope was dead. She had taken her chance, risked all, and lost.

"Oh, little one, if only it were that easy. But I have nothing, and you, ah! You deserve everything." His last word trembled in the air with deep feeling, and he reached out one shaking hand to caress her hair.

"You should have a man with an unstained past, a man with position and money and estates, who could give you jewels and carriages . . . And I . . . I have nothing to give you."

"Does that mean . . ." Her voice quavered. "Does that mean that you like me a l-little?"

"Like you? I lo . . ." He broke off.

"What?" she asked, her breath catching in her throat, her heart thudding sickly. "What were you about to say?"

He shrugged and turned back to the window, and glared out at the scene below. His hands were clenching and unclenching, and with a sudden violent movement he turned and caught her to him in a hard embrace. "My own, my little one, *mon ange,* I love you, I love you. *Je t'adore, ma petite,*" he whispered into her ear, kissing her neck and holding her close. "I never believed in love, but I fell into it, not believing in it. I love you! It is going to kill me to leave you." His voice was hoarse and anguished.

May felt tears coursing down her cheeks and her head spun in absolute joy. "Oh, Etienne!"

His lips closed over hers and she was swirling in a dark, sweet dream, spiraling down into some valley of fragrant flowers and soft sighs. His strong arms surrounded her with his love, and she gave herself up to it. He whispered endearments in French, then in English, and finally reverted wholly to French to express his deepest feelings and desires.

He loved her. She was the cherished one of his heart, and always would be. Every day away from her he would die a little.

Her heart sang in joy, and finally she understood the complex emotions that coursed through her. It was a perfect amalgam of love and desire and tenderness. It was the sweet union of two hearts, two minds, two bodies melding into one even as they kissed and touched and whispered in the darkness.

But at last she awoke from her dream to find herself sitting on his lap in the big leather chair behind Baxter's desk. She had her hands wound around his neck and her fingers in his dark tousled curls. He was silent and still, and she pushed back from his chest so she could look down in his eyes.

"Is that why you would not make love to me when I so shamelessly asked you to? Because you love me?"

He nodded, gazing up at her in the dimness. "Partly. I have never wanted a woman more than I wanted you, but also I knew you were an innocent. To take that innocence, to seduce you, would not have been right, and I loved you too much to do that harm to you."

"I was coming to you to tell you I wasn't a virgin, just so you would make love to me," she said, dreamily. "That was how Dempster caught me out of the house in my night rail. I wanted you so very badly that I was willing to lie to you to have you."

"Ah, my dear, but wanting, needing, desiring are not enough. I say this, I who have made a life's work out of sexual conquest." He took her face in his hands and stared into her blue eyes, plundering their depths for hidden secrets. "I love you. Do you . . ." He released her face. "I have no right to ask," he whispered.

"Ask!" she commanded.

"Do you love me?"

She kissed him firmly on the lips and wiggled back into his arms. She lay against his chest and nuzzled his ear. "How can you even ask? Would I want to make love to you if I did not love you? Of course I love you! I have loved you since that first morning, the ride back to London on Théron."

He was silent.

"Don't you have anything else to say?" she asked, sitting back up and gazing into his eyes, exasperated.

"I do not have the right to ask anything more of you."

She sighed. "You have every right in the world," she urged.

"But I do not."

"Oh, Etienne, you foolish, *foolish* man! Will you marry me? Please, Etienne, will you marry me and make me the happiest woman on earth?"

He swallowed hard and his eyes widened. "Are you sure, my brave little one? I have nothing to give you but my love."

"And I have nothing if you don't give me that. Marry me."

"Yes, my courageous love. Yes, I will marry you."

It was the day she had been waiting for, but now that it was finally here she was as nervous as a green girl at her first ball. Hannah fussed over her, doing up the last pearl buttons on her ivory silk gown and then placing atop her head the wreath of gold and bronze fall flowers that would be her only adornment. Her whole body quivered and she felt like throwing off her gown, finding a pair of breeches and running away with just Cassie for companionship.

What was wrong with her? She was marrying the man she loved in less than an hour in the tiny gray stone chapel on the Brockwith grounds. It was what she wanted. All of her friends and family were there, and Etienne—handsome, gallant, adorable Etienne—was even now donning a gorgeous new suit of blue Bath superfine.

"Leave me for a while Hannah," May said, and as the maid did as she was bid, May stalked over to the window and stood looking blindly out over the Surrey landscape.

Somehow it all seemed so calculated. She had spent the last month attending her mother's wedding, and readying for her own wedding day, standing for innumerable gown fittings, deciding on music, and a menu for the wedding breakfast . . . augh! It had seemed so simple when she asked Etienne to marry her, but then it became immediately complicated with all the details and fuss that every wedding was prey to.

There was a tap at the door behind her and she called, "Come in!"

The door opened and closed, but she could feel no curiosity about who invaded her sanctum.

"I think she is suffering bride nerves; what do you think, Celestine?"

May whirled, to find Emily Delafont and her niece Celestine St. Claire standing inside the door in their wedding finery. Celestine was to stand up with her, and her husband, Justin, was to stand up with Etienne.

Celestine crossed the floor and took May in her arms in a gentle embrace. Her intelligent gray eyes scanned May's face and she nodded. "Bride nerves," she agreed.

Emily joined them by the window. "Do you realize that less than a year ago we were all gathered up north in Cumbria to celebrate Christmas, three 'single' women?"

"You were still married, Aunt, just separated," Celestine protested.

"But I felt single. Baxter and I had not been together as man and wife for seven years! And separated for five; I felt very single, let me assure you. And now I have two babies, Celestine has one, and who knows . . . by next year at this time?" She eyed May with complacency.

"Am I doing the right thing?" May said in a burst of fear. "I always said I would stay single. I always said I was not meant for marriage. . . ."

"Do you love Etienne?" Emily said, gently.

May looked into the eyes of the woman she had thought was her competition for Etienne's affections. "I do. I love him wholly and completely, but is love enough?" She turned her gaze to Celestine. "Is it enough?"

Her friend's calm gray eyes held a thoughtful gleam. She glanced at her aunt. "I will not say that love alone will get you through every trial. Men are incomprehensible sometimes . . . the things they think are important, their fragile sense of self-worth . . ."

May giggled, her nerves bursting to the surface. "Do not tell me that Justin St. Claire is, after all, not perfect?"

"He is perfect in his fallibility," Celestine said, her expression softening. "And he loves me completely. Everything else is just details. If you know Etienne's heart, then you know everything."

Emily nodded. "Listen to us old married ladies, my dear. No matter what arguments and tiffs you two get into—and there will be arguments, my dear, never doubt that—always remember what is in his heart, and appeal to that. He will not fail you."

"But am I doing the right thing?" May clutched at her two friends' arms as a drowning woman going under reaches for a lifeline.

"Trust us," Emily said, glancing over at her niece and then back into May's wide, frightened eyes. "Every bride goes through what you are feeling. Listen to your heart, not your head, right now. If I had listened to my heart, I would have disregarded my hurt feelings when Baxter and I parted, and we could have avoided a long and horrible separation."

May took a deep breath, and the two other women came together with her in a three-way embrace. Listen to my heart, she told herself. Listen to my heart. A calmness descended over her like a benediction from above. She was doing the right thing. She loved Etienne, and he was good for her. She felt like she was really living when she was with him. And she was good for *him*. In the past month they had made such plans for the future! Starting with a honeymoon to France to visit his sisters, and offer them a home in England if they ever needed one.

"I'm ready," she said, pulling out of the warm embrace. "I am ready to get married."

The chapel on the grounds of Brockwith Manor was a tiny gray stone building covered in leafless ivy. Inside, in front of an assembly of friends and relatives, Etienne and May pledged to love each other always as a rare beam of November sun broke through a cloud and lit up the stained glass window behind the altar, sending shards of brilliant color over the congregation. May's mother noisily wept, clinging to the arm of her new husband, a tall, handsome older man that May had liked immediately when they had met at her mother's wedding, and respected, too, when he rejected the money she would have given him as her mother's dowry. He had insisted that she put the money in trust for Maisie.

May's nerves had not completely disappeared. She glanced around at her mother for reassurance, but Maisie's face was buried in Mr. Banks's chest. And then May caught Emily Delafont's eye. The older woman smiled reassuringly and glanced up at her tall, saturnine husband. She squeezed his arm and his expression softened as he gazed down at his plump, pretty wife. Emily caught May's eyes again and nodded.

May understood. Love alone might not be enough, but she knew Etienne's heart, and it was good and true. Together they could weather any storm.

Night closed in early so late in November. When May and Etienne's carriage pulled up to an inn halfway between Surrey and Dover, the inn in which they would spend their first night as man and wife, it had already been dark for hours. Only the coach's lamps and dim moonlight that peeked out from behind clouds had lit their way.

The wedding breakfast had been hilarious, with laughter from one end of the long table to the other. There had been speeches and toasts, anecdotes and a little ribald kidding, interrupted by the various needs of the babies—Celestine and Justin's son, and Emily and Baxter's son and daughter. Etienne and Justin had become fast friends, after a wary few minutes when they first met. Both men were possessed of a devastating charm with the ladies, but were quite happy with their fates as married men. And each was convinced that his horse was the fastest, bravest beast in England. It was agreed that the next summer there would be a definitive race between Etienne on Théron and Justin on Alphonse to settle the matter.

May's faith in Baxter Delafont and his rigid code of honor turned out to be justified. He had investigated Etienne's branch of the Delafont family in the month before May's wedding, and had found that Etienne's great-grandfather had left England and never claimed an inheritance that was owed him. It had been accumulating interest ever since and was now a considerable sum. Etienne was rich. Perhaps even richer than May, but no one was counting. Ironically, he could have had it just for the asking, any time, if he had just declared himself to Baxter years before.

Also in the month between proposal and wedding they had found out that Cassie was "with foal," as May laughingly called it, with Théron the proud father. It was the very beginning of the magnificent plans May and her new husband had for a stud farm. Though their plans would have to wait just awhile longer, as they had *other* plans to bring to fruition, among them, the honeymoon.

But now May was alone with Etienne in their room at the inn, a comfortable, warm, lovely room, but only one. "It is all we will need," Etienne had said, with the banked fire in his eyes leaping into flame whenever he mentioned their wedding night.

May sat on the edge of the high bed, waiting, as Etienne changed out of his clothes in the adjoined dressing room. Finally he entered, wearing a dressing gown given to him, with much laughter, by his cousin the marquess. Baxter had said, with quirked eyebrows, that it was one piece of clothing that would likely stay good for years, for it never would stay on for more than a few minutes at a time. Dodo, present when her nephew had said such a scandalous thing, had swatted him much as she might have when he was a little boy, but had laughed nonetheless, as had everyone else.

May swallowed hard, but gazed steadily at her handsome husband . . . husband! How strange to even think the word, when she had sworn never to marry. And yet every morning since her proposal to Etienne she had awoken with the knowledge that she was the luckiest woman alive. The firelight flickered over the rich burgundy of the dressing gown and over his bare legs. Eyes wide, she gazed down at his naked limbs as she slipped off the bed and stood, uncertain what she should do.

"Are you frightened, little one?" he asked, the firelight glinting on the mahogany flecks in his tawny eyes.

"A little," she whispered. She felt such a welter of emotions—fear, desire, nervousness, love, anticipation—that she hardly knew which was strongest.

He moved toward her but stood still several feet away. Tenderness shone from his eyes. "I . . . I will wait, if you are too frightened. Always, *mon ange,* you must tell me what you want and what you need from me, and I will do my best to fulfill your desires. I will go as slowly as you need me to."

"No!" she blurted out, and then felt the blush rise through her body at her eagerness. "No, I want . . . I want . . ." She could not say what she wanted, but she had dreamt of it many times. She would not put off this night for anything, for the moment was coming when they would be truly wedded, finally as one.

He smiled, a secret smile of satisfaction. "Then come to me, my love," he whispered.

As if in a dream, she floated across the few feet that separated them and stood before him, looking up into his eyes with trust and adoration. He was hers for all time! How was this possible? she wondered. After they found that he was rich, her deepest fear was that he would cry off, that he was marrying her as the only alternative to penury. Her expression of that fear had resulted in their only fight so far, and she knew that he had been hurt by her worry.

She had spent days in an agony of fear that she had hurt him so deeply that his love would turn cold, but after a while she realized that he had forgiven her, and he never said another word about it. He loved her. That was the only reason a man like him would ever marry, and she must know that, he said finally, when she brought it up once again. He forgave her for her doubt because he knew in his heart his own motives for marrying her, and knew that in time she would understand how much he loved her.

She did. How it had happened she had no idea, but she knew in that instant that he really loved her. What he never said, but what she felt he understood, was that her fear of him leaving her had more to do with her own self-doubt, and that his love would gradually heal that part of her. Already the healing had begun.

And now she stood before him as his wife. He kissed her ear, whispering naughty things to her in French to make her blush, and then his trembling fingers untied the front of her night rail as he trailed kisses down her neck. He pushed her gown over her shoulders and it fell in a puddle of sheer fabric at her feet.

He took one step back and she shivered in the coolness of the room, afraid of what she would see in his eyes, any hint of disappointment, but as he gazed over her body his eyes lit with an inner glow. "You are perfect!" he whispered, taking a deep, shuddering breath. He reached out one hand and touched the birthmark on her breast, and then cupped it with a gentle hand. "*Absolument parfait. Ravissant!*"

Her whole body convulsed at this first touch on her naked skin by her husband. He had told her so much, taught her so much, that she knew her body was ready that very moment to receive him, but she also knew that he would take his time in his oh, so skillful way. It would be exquisite torture. For him, too, she hoped.

But there was still one nagging doubt in her mind. Should she say it? Would she ruin this perfect moment with her doubts and fear? But in the end she could not restrain herself. "But, Etienne, you like . . . you like more ample women, I *know* you do. Women like Emily."

"I have changed my mind," he said and smiled at her, shaking back the dark curls that framed his face. "I find myself entranced by a lithe, slim, perfect little one. A wood nymph with auburn hair that glows like fire and with eyes the color of the sky over the channel. A woman who is . . . how do you English say this? Ah, 'pluck to the backbone' is my little one. Brave enough, even, to propose to and wed a naughty Frenchman without a sou to his name."

He advanced on her and swung her up in his arms and carried her to the bed, setting her gently down on the covers and placing one warm kiss on her flat stomach before straightening up.

"Will you change your mind back?" May asked.

Eyes wide, she watched him shrug out of the dressing gown, not so much as a nightshirt underneath. The firelight danced over his naked skin and she licked her suddenly dry lips as she let her gaze wander over his body until it was riveted on the evidence that he wanted her very much.

He lay down on the bed beside her and caressed her, letting his hands wander over her slim curves until she felt her body ignite, and she was no longer cold, but fevered with desire. He pulled her close and she felt the hard contours of his body mold her to his will. Soon she would be possessed by this glorious man, she thought as she let her own hands wander, and heard him gasp as she dared so much more than she would have believed she ever could. Her fingers traced the scar on his hip, so close to his groin, now a healed memory of their time together in her folly.

"I will never change my mind about you, little one," he said, his words muttered hoarsely. "From now until the end of time you will be my measure of perfection in all things, including the sweetness of your body, which now, if you do not mind, I will sample."

He bent his head and kissed and nibbled his way over her skin, and soon they were both lost to every thought but that they loved and wanted each other.

Much later, under the warm covers of their nuptial bed, Etienne slumbered and May drowsed near sleep, nestled in his arms. So that was what she had so feared, she thought, feeling the change in her body wrought by marriage. She felt very, *very* married now, and gloried in it. Miss Parsons was so very wrong about lovemaking. She moved luxuriously, sinuously, rubbing herself shamelessly against her lover's hard body and knew the moment Etienne was awake again. She felt the pulse of desire shudder through him.

Without a word, he pulled her to him and kissed her softly on the lips, then disappeared under the covers. May giggled and then gasped, as her husband did scandalous things to her body. Poor Miss Parsons, to have missed this wonder, this ecstasy. . . .

And then any thought of anyone else in the world but her husband was lost.

"Oh, Etienne!" She gasped, lost in a delicious whirl of love. He pulled her under the covers and silenced her in the sweetest of ways.

ABOUT THE AUTHOR

Donna Simpson lives with her family in Canada. She is currently working on her next Zebra regency romance, *Miss Truelove Beckons,* to be published in June 2001. Donna loves to hear from readers and you may write to her c/o Zebra Books. Please include a self-addressed stamped envelope if you wish a reply.

BOOK YOUR PLACE ON OUR WEBSITE
AND MAKE THE
READING CONNECTION!

We've created a customized website just for our very special readers, where you can get the inside scoop on everything that's going on with Zebra, Pinnacle and Kensington books.

When you come online, you'll have the exciting opportunity to:

- View covers of upcoming books
- Read sample chapters
- Learn about our future publishing schedule (listed by publication month *and author*)
- Find out when your favorite authors will be visiting a city near you
- Search for and order backlist books from our online catalog
- Check out author bios and background information
- Send e-mail to your favorite authors
- Meet the Kensington staff online
- Join us in weekly chats with authors, readers and other guests
- Get writing guidelines
- AND MUCH MORE!

**Visit our website at
http://www.zebrabooks.com**

More Zebra Regency Romances